S0-APQ-763

JOIN THE FUN
IN CABIN SIX . . .

KATIE is the perfect team player. She loves competitive games, planned activities, and coming up with her own great ideas.

MEGAN would rather lose herself in fantasyland than get into organized fun.

SARAH would be much happier if she could spend her time reading instead of exerting herself.

ERIN is much more interested in boys, clothes, and makeup than in playing kids' games at camp.

TRINA hates conflicts. She just wants everyone to be happy . . .

AND THEY ARE! Despite all their differences, the Cabin Six bunch are having the time of their lives at CAMP SUNNYSIDE!

Look for More Fun and Games with
CAMP SUNNYSIDE FRIENDS
by Marilyn Kaye
from Avon Books

(#1) NO BOYS ALLOWED!
(#2) CABIN SIX PLAYS CUPID
(#3) COLOR WAR!
(#4) NEW GIRL IN CABIN SIX
(#5) LOOKING FOR TROUBLE
(#6) KATIE STEALS THE SHOW
(#7) A WITCH IN CABIN SIX
(#8) TOO MANY COUNSELORS
(#9) THE NEW-AND-IMPROVED SARAH
(#10) ERIN AND THE MOVIE STAR
(#11) THE PROBLEM WITH PARENTS
(#12) THE TENNIS TRAP
(#13) BIG SISTER BLUES

And Don't Forget to Pick Up . . .

CAMP SUNNYSIDE FRIENDS SPECIAL: CHRISTMAS REUNION

Coming Soon

(#15) CHRISTMAS BREAK

MARILYN KAYE is the author of many popular books for young readers, including the "Out of This World" series and the "Sisters" books. She is an associate professor at St. John's University and lives in Brooklyn, New York.

Camp Sunnyside is the camp Marilyn Kaye wishes that she had gone to every summer when she was a kid.

Avon Books are available at special quantity discounts for bulk purchases for sales promotions, premiums, fund raising or educational use. Special books, or book excerpts, can also be created to fit specific needs.

For details write or telephone the office of the Director of Special Markets, Avon Books, Dept. FP, 1350 Avenue of the Americas, New York, New York 10019, 1-800-238-0658.

Megan's Ghost

Marilyn Kaye

AN AVON  CAMELOT BOOK

If you purchased this book without a cover, you should be aware that this book is stolen property. It was reported as "unsold and destroyed" to the publisher, and neither the author nor the publisher has received any payment for this "stripped book."

CAMP SUNNYSIDE FRIENDS #14: MEGAN'S GHOST is an original publication of Avon Books. This work has never before appeared in book form.

AVON BOOKS
A division of
The Hearst Corporation
1350 Avenue of the Americas
New York, New York 10019

Copyright © 1991 by Marilyn Kaye
Published by arrangement with the author
Library of Congress Catalog Card Number: 91-92048
ISBN: 0-380-76552-7
RL: 4.8

All rights reserved, which includes the right to reproduce this book or portions thereof in any form whatsoever except as provided by the U.S. Copyright Law. For information address Writers House Inc., 21 West 26th Street, New York, New York 10010.

First Avon Camelot Printing: October 1991

CAMELOT TRADEMARK REG. U.S. PAT. OFF. AND IN OTHER COUNTRIES, MARCA REGISTRADA, HECHO EN U.S.A.

Printed in the U.S.A.

OPM 10 9 8 7 6 5 4 3 2 1

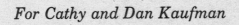

For Cathy and Dan Kaufman

CAMP SUNNYSIDE FRIENDS #14

Chapter 1

"Megan! Stop dawdling and come eat your breakfast!"

Her mother's voice floated into the bedroom where Megan Lindsay sat on her bed. Although her mind was far away, the words slowly penetrated her head. She folded the sheet of stationery she held and stuffed it in her back pocket. Passing the mirror, she glanced to see if she'd remembered to brush her hair. Not that it made much difference one way or the other. Her wild red curls always looked the same.

"Good morning," she sang out as she entered the kitchen. Her father peered over his coffee cup and winked a greeting. In his high chair, her baby brother, Alex, bounced up and down, the way he always did when he saw Megan. And her mother gazed at her with an expression that combined affection and exasperation.

1

"Good morning, honey," she said. "It's about time!"

Megan took her seat. "About time for what, Mom?"

"It's about time you decided to join us." Mrs. Lindsay poured juice from a pitcher into Megan's glass.

Megan plunged into her scrambled eggs. "I came when you called me."

"The third time she called you," her father pointed out.

"Really? You called me three times?" Megan helped herself to bacon. "I didn't hear you."

"How strange," her father noted dryly.

Megan couldn't help grinning. Her tendency to daydream and block out all sounds was well-known. "Sorry. I was reading the letter I got from Sarah."

"Again?" Her mother smiled. "You got that letter three days ago."

"Sarah's letters are like great stories you can read over and over," Megan told her. "Maybe that's because she reads so much. She really knows how to write." She pulled the letter out of her pocket and opened it.

"Megan, sweetie, not at the table," her mother reprimanded her gently.

Sighing, Megan replaced it. She didn't really

need to read it again. By now, she pretty much knew it by heart.

The best part was Sarah's description of a visit she'd made with her father to a carnival. It was amazing—they'd run into Trina Sandburg and her mother there! The way Sarah described their ride on the gigantic roller coaster, Megan could almost feel herself going up and down and around and getting just as dizzy as Sarah said she'd been. And she could share Sarah's surprise and excitement at meeting Trina.

"Megan, those eggs are going to get cold," her father warned.

"I miss them," Megan murmured.

Her parents exchanged puzzled looks. "You miss your eggs?" her mother asked.

Megan giggled. "No. I miss Sarah and Trina and all the other cabin six kids. It's funny. I've only been away from Camp Sunnyside for two months and it feels like years since I've seen those guys."

"You could always visit them," her mother said. "Or you could invite them to come here. None of the girls lives very far away, do they?"

"Two hours at the most," Megan admitted. "But there's never any time! I've got my tennis lessons and piano lessons, and Ms. Devlin piles on the homework. It's hard to find time to hang out with my friends right here in town! Of course, if I could give up piano . . ." She eyed her parents hopefully.

Mr. Lindsay acted like he was considering that. Then he grinned. "Why not give up tennis instead?"

"Dad!" Megan rolled her eyes. How could he even think of such a thing? Or compare playing tennis with playing the piano? Tennis was her passion, her absolutely number one favorite activity. Piano was just plain drudgery.

She was draining her juice when she heard a familiar shout from outside. "Megan!"

Hurriedly, Megan wiped her mouth with a napkin. "Have a nice day," her parents chorused. Megan paused to plant a kiss on her baby brother's forehead and blow kisses to her parents. Then she grabbed her jacket from the hall closet, snatched up her knapsack, and ran outside.

A slender girl with long, straight brown hair was waiting on the front porch. "Hurry up," she said as Megan struggled into her jacket. "You know what will happen if we're late."

Megan didn't want to stay after school any more than Krista did. "I'm zipping as fast as I can," she replied. Together, they headed to the sidewalk.

This was their regular routine. Whoever was ready to leave for school first stopped at the other's house and yelled. It was usually Krista calling for Megan, since Megan was always running late. She was definitely lucky having a best friend who lived right next door, or she'd never get to school on time.

"Look at that tree," Krista said as they walked. "It's like the leaves are real gold."

"Mm, I love the fall." Megan took a deep breath of the crisp October air.

"I can't wait for winter," Krista said. "Ice-skating, skiing, Christmas . . ."

"And then comes spring," Megan continued. "That's *my* favorite season."

"Why?"

"The state tennis tournament!"

Krista slapped her own forehead. "Stupid me. How could I forget that? It's all you talked about last spring!"

"Of course, summer's great too," Megan mused. "I wish you could come to Camp Sunnyside, Krista. It's so cool. I've got the neatest cabin mates."

"I know, I know," Krista declared. "I've only been hearing about them for three years."

"I just got a letter from Sarah Fine last Friday," Megan told her.

"Sarah's the one who has the bunk above yours, right? The one who reads all the time?"

Megan nodded. "She went to a carnival last week and saw Trina Sandburg there."

"Trina Sandburg," Krista repeated. "Is she the rich, pretty one?"

"No, that's Erin Chapman. Trina's the one who's sweet and settles everyone's arguments. She's got the bunk below Katie Dillon."

"Oh yeah, Katie. She's the bossy one."

Megan thought about that. "Well, she's not exactly bossy. She just likes to take charge of whatever's going on."

"I've heard so much about them, I feel like I already know them," Krista said. "I wish I could meet them sometime."

"Maybe you will," Megan replied. "Hey, did you get all those math problems done?"

Krista made a face. "Yeah, but it took me forever. I think Ms. Devlin gives more homework than any other sixth grade teacher at school. And she's so strict about rules."

Megan agreed fervently. "But I like her anyway. At least she's always fair and she doesn't have class favorites."

Krista nodded. "Yeah, I'd hate to be in a class where the teacher has pets."

"Me too," Megan said. "Unless *we* were the pets!"

They both giggled as they passed the church and the small cemetery next to it. Then Krista stopped giggling suddenly, and shivered.

"Are you cold?" Megan asked.

"No. It's that house." She glanced at the old, run-down place set way back from the road and up the hill. "It always gives me the creeps."

Megan had to admit that she sometimes had the same feeling when she passed it too. The house had a very gloomy look about it.

"You don't think it's true, do you?" Krista asked. "What they say about that house?"

"What do they say?"

"That it's haunted, and there's a real ghost inside."

"Don't be silly," Megan said, but her tone lacked confidence. "There's no such thing as ghosts."

"Oh, I don't believe in ghosts either," Krista quickly assured her. "But I heard that sometimes people see a light go on and off, up on the second floor. And a lady behind the window."

"I don't believe that," Megan stated. "That house has been empty for almost a year. And I'll bet it stays empty too. Who would ever want to move into that ugly old place?"

7

"Someone's moving into the house across the street," Krista noted.

Megan turned. Sure enough, there were big moving vans parked in front of the grand, old Victorian house on the opposite side of the road. The girls stood there and gaped at the men carrying things into it.

"Wow, get a load of that table," Krista murmured. "And a grand piano!"

"Did you see the size of that television?" Megan thought it looked more like a movie screen.

"And a bed with a canopy!" Krista squealed. "They must be rich, whoever they are."

"Maybe they're famous, like movie stars," Megan suggested. "Wouldn't that be neat, having movie stars living just a few blocks away? Or rock stars!"

"Oh, Megan, you're letting your imagination run away again," Krista scoffed. "Movie stars and rock stars don't live in small towns in Pennsylvania."

For several more minutes, the girls watched in awe at the fancy items being taken into the house. Then, from the church they had just passed, came the ringing of chimes that sounded every hour.

8

"Ohmigosh, we're going to be late!" Krista yelped.

They ran the rest of the way to school. Just as they entered the building, a bell rang. "Oh no," Megan moaned. "We're in trouble."

But luck was with them. As they dashed into their classroom, they saw that Ms. Devlin wasn't at her desk. With a sigh of relief, Megan slid into her desk and Krista sat down next to her. In every class they'd been in since first grade they always started the year sitting side by side. Usually, within a few weeks, the teacher split them up for talking too much. But here it was October already, and they hadn't been separated. Either they'd become much better at whispering, or Ms. Devlin was a lot less strict than she appeared to be.

The classroom door opened, and the school secretary stuck her head in. "Boys and girls, Ms. Devlin will be here in a few minutes. Please remain in your seats and read quietly."

Naturally, the second she disappeared, everyone started moving about and talking. Two girls came over to Megan and Krista.

"Boy, you guys lucked out," Paige said.

"Yeah, you know how Ms. Devlin hates tardiness," Julie added.

"What were you doing anyway?" Paige asked.

"We were hanging around in front of the old house by the cemetery, watching movers," Krista told them.

Julie's eyes widened and she gasped. "Someone's moving into that old haunted house?"

Megan rolled her eyes. "It's not haunted."

"That's not where the movers were," Krista said. "Someone's moving into the house across the street. You know, the big fancy one."

"Oh. Well, speaking of haunted houses," Julie began, but Megan interrupted her.

"It's *not* haunted!"

Julie shrugged. "Okay, okay. But anyway, what are we going to do about Halloween?"

"Gee, I haven't even thought about Halloween," Megan said.

"It's only two weeks away," Paige noted.

"Why can't we just go trick-or-treating, like we usually do," Krista suggested.

Paige wrinkled her nose. "That's so babyish."

She had a point, Megan thought. "But it's fun to dress up in a costume. And you can't do that unless you go trick-or-treating."

"Maybe one of us could have a party instead," Krista suggested.

But before they could consider that, the classroom door opened again. Julie and Paige scurried back to their seats.

Ms. Devlin wasn't alone. Megan gazed curiously at the pretty, fair-haired girl who followed the teacher into the room. There was something familiar about her. Megan racked her brain, trying to think where she'd seen her before.

Ms. Devlin stood before the class and placed a hand on the girl's shoulder. "Class, this is Lori Landers. Lori's family has just moved here, and she's joining our class. I know you'll all do your best to make her feel welcome."

Lori Landers, Lori Landers . . . the name rang a bell in Megan's head. Then she remembered. Lori had been at the state tennis tournament last spring! It all came back to her in a rush. There had been a lot of girls there from all over the state, and most of them had become nothing more than a blur in her memory. But Lori stood out.

She'd been one of the best tennis players there, and Megan recalled admiring her talent. She'd never had a chance to really talk to Lori, but she clearly remembered watching her play in the semifinals and thinking about what a tough opponent she'd be. She had excellent form.

She wasn't better than Megan, though. Me-

11

gan beat Lori in the finals. But it hadn't been easy. In fact, it had been one of the toughest and most challenging matches Megan had ever played in. Lori played a fierce game, and it had taken all of Megan's skill and concentration to win.

And now Lori would be living right here in town! A wave of excitement shot through her. It was hard finding kids her age to play serious tennis with, here at home. Megan never had to play very hard to beat them. Maybe she and Lori could start playing regularly!

"Lori, there's an empty seat right behind Krista," Ms. Devlin was saying. "Krista, raise your hand."

As the girl proceeded down the aisle, Megan looked at her and smiled. But Lori didn't respond, even though she seemed to be looking right at her. Maybe she doesn't remember me, Megan thought.

When Lori took her seat, Megan turned and faced her directly. "Hi!" she whispered. This time, there was no mistaking the look of recognition on Lori's face. Her cool green eyes met Megan's. But she didn't smile.

She's probably shy, Megan decided. It must feel icky, being the new girl at school and not knowing anyone. Well, Megan could take care

12

of that soon enough. As soon as lunch time came around, she'd take Lori under her wing. She'd help her out, introduce her to all the kids, and make sure she felt welcome here, just like Ms. Devlin asked them to.

It was the least she could do for a tennis pal.

Chapter 2

"Class, line up for lunch," Ms. Devlin announced at noon. Along with everyone else, Megan rose and stood by her desk. The class filed out of the room in rows, and while Megan waited for the row to the right of her to leave, she took the opportunity to look at Lori again.

Lori was looking at her. Ms. Devlin didn't like them to talk while in line, so Megan couldn't say anything to her. But she did give Lori a warm, encouraging smile. Once again, Lori didn't return it.

She's really nervous about being here, Megan thought sympathetically. She's afraid we're all going to be unfriendly snobs or something. As soon as they got out of the cafeteria line with their trays, she would invite the new girl to join her group at their table.

14

The class walked down the hall and into the cafeteria. When Megan emerged from the line, she went to her usual table, where Krista, Julie, and Paige were already sitting. Megan put her tray down, but she remained standing and watched as her classmates came out.

"What are you waiting for?" Paige asked.

"I'm looking for Lori," Megan replied.

"Who?" Julie asked.

"The new girl. I sort of know her. She was at the tennis tournament last spring."

"She's back there," Krista told her. "She didn't go through the line. I guess she brought her lunch."

Julie giggled as Megan peered toward the back of the room. There was Lori, all alone, with a lunch box. Oh dear, she thought. The poor girl didn't know that it was considered very uncool to bring a lunch in the sixth grade.

"Check out that sweater she's wearing," Paige directed.

"What about it?" Megan asked.

"I saw it in the window of a store last week. It's unbelievably expensive."

It looked like an ordinary sweater to Megan, but Paige was into clothes so she was probably right.

Krista turned and eyed the girl with interest. "Megan, maybe she's the one who moved into that big house. Is she rich?"

Megan shrugged. "All I know is that she's a super tennis player." And probably lonely, she thought. "I think we should ask her to come sit with us."

Krista agreed. "I'll go with you." The two of them walked over to the table where Lori was sitting, taking several small containers out of her lunch box.

"Hi," Megan said brightly. "Remember me? I'm Megan Lindsay. We were at the tennis tournament last spring."

"I remember you," Lori replied. But her face was blank.

"This is Krista McGowan," Megan continued.

Lori's expression changed completely. "Hi, Krista! Nice to meet you."

"Would you like to come sit with us?" Krista asked.

"I'd love to," Lori replied promptly. She gathered up her containers and put them back in the lunch box. Then she followed Megan and Krista.

"This is Lori," Megan said to the others. "Lori, that's Paige and Julie." Lori greeted each of them nicely, and sat down.

"There were some movers in front of a house on Oak Street this morning," Krista told Lori. "Is that where you're living?"

Lori nodded. "It's not as big as the house we used to live in, but I think it's okay."

"We saw the movers bring in a canopy bed," Krista said. "Is that yours?"

"Yes. And I have a vanity table with a ruffle that matches it."

"Wow," Paige breathed. "A canopy bed. I always wanted one of those."

"I just hope the movers don't break any of my things," Lori said with a sigh.

"What kind of things?" Julie asked.

"Well, my television and my stereo, for example."

Julie's eyebrows shot up. "You have your own television and stereo?"

"Yes. My own telephone, too."

Paige sighed. "I wish my parents would put an extension in my room."

"Oh, it's not an extension," Lori told her. "It's my own private phone. I'll know the number by tomorrow."

Krista gazed at her with unconcealed envy. To Megan, it sounded like Lori was showing off. She was probably trying to impress them

17

all. Personally, Megan thought Lori's bragging was just going to turn them off.

But that didn't seem to be the case. They were all gazing at her in fascination.

"But how do you feel about living right across the street from a haunted house?" Julie asked.

Megan groaned. Julie could be so silly sometimes. She might really scare Lori. "It's not haunted," she assured Lori. "That's just a silly story. Don't even think about it."

Lori acted like she hadn't even heard Megan. She leaned across the table toward Julie. "Tell me more! Is it really haunted?"

"That's what everyone says," Julie told her. "Some people moved in there about a year ago. They were going to fix the place up. But then, all of a sudden, they left."

"People said a ghost scared them away," Paige added.

Megan fidgeted uneasily. She'd heard those stories too. And she'd always tried very hard not to believe them. The idea of a ghost made her skin crawl.

But Lori didn't appear to be upset by the story. "Wow, that's wild!" As she opened one of her little containers, she glanced at what the

18

others had on their plates. "Ick, I see that the food here isn't any better than what we got at my old school. How can you eat it?"

"It *is* pretty disgusting," Krista admitted. "But . . ." she hesitated and glanced at Megan.

Megan felt that it was up to her to put Lori straight on what was in and what was out. "Maybe it was different at your old school, but here, after fourth grade, no one brings lunch from home," she said kindly. "I guess you couldn't have known that."

Lori gave Megan only the briefest of glances, and directed her reply to the others. "It wouldn't make any difference if I had known. What's the point of eating disgusting school food if you can bring something nice?"

Julie peered into Lori's container. "What is that, anyway?"

"It's a cold pasta salad," Lori replied. "Would you like a bite?" She passed the container to Julie, who stuck her fork into it.

"Mm, that's great!"

"You can all try it," Lori said. Julie passed the container around, and each girl exclaimed over it. Just as Krista was about to pass it to Megan, Lori snatched it back.

"That's okay," Megan said quickly. "You want to have some left for yourself!"

19

But once again, Lori didn't even acknowledge her.

"By the way, I love your sweater," Paige said.

Lori preened. "Thank you. I just got it last month. In fact, this is only the second time I've worn it. The first time I wore it was to the New Kids on the Block concert."

Julie, Krista, and Megan squealed. "Did you really see them in person?" Krista gasped.

"I just adore them," Paige moaned.

"I didn't just see them," Lori said. "I *met* them."

Gasps of astonishment, amazement, and disbelief greeted this announcement.

"You see," Lori explained, "I had this friend whose father works for a record company. And he got us special passes to go backstage after the concert and meet them. I had my picture taken with them."

The gasps were turning into little shrieks.

"I just got their new album," Megan began, but Lori went right on talking as if Megan weren't there.

"One of them put his arm around me."

The little shrieks became big ones. "Which one?" Julie asked.

"Was it Jordan?" Krista hugged herself and sighed.

Ms. Devlin appeared by their table. "Girls! A little less noise, please! It's time to get back to class."

Megan rose with the others, and they lined up to go back. Once in the classroom, Ms. Devlin began the math lesson. Usually, Megan paid close attention, since math wasn't her best subject. But today, she found it hard to concentrate. She was thinking about Lori.

Was it just her imagination, or was Lori being a lot less friendly to her than she was to the other girls? Megan thought it would be the opposite way. After all, even though they weren't friends, she'd met Megan before. And they had something major in common, tennis. It was funny, too, that Lori hadn't even mentioned tennis.

"Megan!"

Megan blinked. "Yes?"

"I've called on you twice!" Ms. Devlin said. "Please try to pay attention."

"I'm sorry," Megan said meekly. From behind her, she heard the unmistakable sound of a giggle. She glanced back. Lori was smirking.

Megan was bewildered. This was really weird. What was Lori's problem, anyway?

21

Could it have something to do with the tournament last spring? Maybe Lori was uncomfortable, seeing Megan again after having been defeated. Maybe she felt intimidated by Megan, or she was afraid Megan was the kind of person who would make fun of the way Lori played.

Megan decided she was just going to have to be especially nice to her. She'd show Lori that she wasn't stuck up, and she didn't have a swollen head about winning or anything like that. She'd invite Lori to play tennis with her this weekend. And maybe she'd even lose to Lori, just to make her feel better.

She had a chance to talk to the new girl in phys. ed. They were changing in the locker room, and Megan approached her. "You know, we've got good tennis courts at the community center here. I play there practically every Saturday."

"Good for you," Lori said.

"You want to play with me this Saturday?"

"No."

Krista was standing on her other side. "Megan said you're a good tennis player."

Megan waited for Lori to thank her for the compliment, but Lori just turned her back on

Megan and smiled at Krista. "I don't play tennis anymore. I'm into ballet now."

"I take ballet too!" Krista exclaimed. "Are you on pointe yet?"

As the two of them started chattering about ballet, Megan slunk away. This didn't make any sense at all. Why would a good tennis player stop playing tennis?

She didn't want to dwell on the mystery of Lori all day. But it was impossible not to. She tried to remember exactly what had happened at the state tournament. Had she said something unkind to Lori, something that would make her want to quit playing tennis? No, she couldn't remember talking to her at all. Could Lori have had some sort of injury that stopped her from playing anymore? No, that wasn't possible. If she had an injury, she wouldn't be able to dance.

"Megan!"

Megan gulped. "Uh, could you repeat the question, Ms. Devlin?"

"Megan, if you would pay attention, I wouldn't have to repeat it." The teacher's voice was gentle but firm.

Once again, she heard that titter coming from Lori. Megan tried to ignore it and concentrate

23

on the teacher. Ms. Devlin had already spoken to her once about not paying attention. So she pushed this puzzling situation out of her head for the time being, and somehow managed to get through the rest of the day without being caught with her mind elsewhere.

When the bell rang at the end of the day, she rose with the others. But instead of leaving, she whispered "Wait for me," to Krista, and broke out of the line to go to the teacher's desk.

"I'm sorry I was so out of it today, Ms. Devlin. I'll try not to daydream in class."

Ms. Devlin smiled at her. "I know you will, Megan. And I accept your apology."

Megan thanked her and hurried out to the hall. There, she saw Krista and her other friends looking very excited. "Lori's invited us over to her house to see her New Kids on the Block picture!"

"Cool!" Megan exclaimed. Then she remembered something and her face fell. "Oh, darn. I've got piano." She looked around. "Where is Lori?"

"She went into the rest room," Paige said.

Megan went across the hall and into the rest room. Lori was standing in front of the mirror, brushing her long blonde hair.

"Lori, I'm sorry, but I've got a dumb piano lesson this afternoon. So I can't come over."

Lori dropped her brush into her pocketbook and went to the door. She paused before opening it, then spoke.

"I didn't invite *you.*"

Chapter 3

"Megan, we had so much fun!" Krista declared in rapture as she and Megan walked to school the next day. "You should have been there."

Megan didn't want to tell her that she hadn't been invited. "What's her house like inside?"

"Fantastic! Lori's room is outrageous. She's got *everything*. She even has her own VCR! We saw the picture of her with the New Kids on the Block. I thought I was going to faint!"

Megan felt a twinge of envy. She would have liked to see that. "What else did you guys do?" She was panting slightly as she spoke. They were walking faster than usual, remembering their narrow escape from detention yesterday.

"We watched some videos, and then Lori's mother called us down for a snack. I thought it would just be cookies and stuff like that, but

26

she'd gone to a bakery. We had all these fancy cakes and eclairs. I stuffed myself!"

Megan's mouth was watering. But there was something else she was more interested in knowing. "Did . . . did Lori say anything about me?"

"Like what?"

"I don't know." Megan hesitated. "I don't think she likes me very much."

Krista looked perplexed. "Why wouldn't she like you?"

Megan kicked at a stone. "Well, I did beat her in that tennis tournament."

"That was five months ago," Krista scoffed. "Nobody holds a grudge that long."

"I know that," Megan said. "But I'm not sure Lori does."

"Did she say anything to you about it?"

"Not exactly . . ."

"That's just your imagination," Krista assured her. "It's all in your head. You know how you make things up."

Megan gave her a halfhearted nod. Krista was right about that. But she didn't think Lori's attitude was just one of her fantasies.

"Lori's *neat*," Krista went on. "She's got lots of personality, and she's so generous. Paige was oohing and ahhing over some scarf in Lori's closet, and Lori insisted on giving it to her. And she showed Julie how to put her hair in a French braid."

"That's amazing."

Krista must have detected the slight note of sarcasm in Megan's voice, because she glanced at her suspiciously. Megan tried to keep her face a blank. But then she noticed something out of the ordinary.

Krista was carrying a brown bag.

"What's that?"

"My lunch."

"You're bringing your lunch to school?"

"Yeah."

Megan groaned. "Honestly, Krista. Just because Lori brings her lunch to school, that doesn't mean it's suddenly the cool thing to do."

Krista immediately defended herself. "That's not why I'm doing it. I was thinking about what Lori said yesterday. It doesn't make sense, eating that school garbage. So this morning I made myself a bologna sandwich, and I've got some potato chips and a banana."

Which would be a whole lot better than whatever they'd be fed at school, Megan had to admit.

"It sounds to me like you're the one who doesn't like Lori," Krista added.

"I didn't say that," Megan protested. She thought hard. Maybe she *hadn't* heard Lori right yesterday. No, she had definitely said Megan wasn't invited. But maybe she was just offended when Megan had told her she couldn't come over, and that's why she'd acted so mean.

"Good," Krista said. "Because we invited her to go to the mall with us Saturday."

Going to the mall on Saturdays had become a tradition during the past year. On Saturday morning, Megan played tennis at the community center. Then her mother or her father picked her up and dropped her at the mall, where she met Krista, Paige, and Julie for lunch at Burger Bonanza.

"That's nice," Megan said. Actually, the more she thought about it, the better the idea sounded. Lori would *have* to talk to her there, or the others would be bound to notice and decide that maybe Lori wasn't so neat after all.

"Lori's parents are building a swimming pool in their backyard," Krista told her. "It's going to be ready by the time the weather gets warm. Lori says she's going to have swimming parties every weekend."

"That's what she *says,*" Megan murmured. "You don't know if it's true. Maybe she's just showing off, to impress us."

Krista frowned. "Why would she do that? Honestly, Megan, you sound like you're jealous. You should be more open-minded about Lori."

Megan thought Krista's tone was annoying. She was lecturing Megan as if Megan was a child.

They actually arrived at school early. "Oh, great," Krista said, noticing the time on the hallway clock. "I'm going to class and try to get the rest of these math problems done."

"I have to return a book to the library," Megan told her. "I'll see you in a few minutes."

The library was quiet. Megan returned her book, and she was just about to leave when she saw Lori. She debated to herself. Maybe Krista was right, and she should be more open-minded about Lori. If Krista, Julie, and Paige were going to be friends with her, Megan had to make every possible effort to do the same. And this was a good opportunity to strike up a conversation. The librarian didn't mind if people talked as long as they spoke quietly.

"Hi," Megan said. "How do you like it here so far?"

It was a direct question. Lori *had* to reply. And she did. She mumbled something that sounded like "It's okay."

Encouraged, Megan continued. "I'm glad you like my friends. They're all really cool."

That got no response at all. But Megan wasn't going to give up. She just kept on talking. "Krista's my best friend. We've known each other since kindergarten. I remember when our mothers took us shopping when we were five. We both wanted the same teddy bear, but there was only one in the store. I think that's the only time we ever had a real fight!"

Lori still didn't say anything, but Megan could tell she was listening. So she went on. "We made such a fuss that the store manager felt sorry for us. He called all these other stores until he found one that had the same bear! Right then and there, Krista and I made a pledge that we'd always sleep with our teddy bears, forever and ever."

Lori turned and looked at her. She actually appeared to be interested in this story. "Do you still sleep with your teddy bear?"

Megan laughed. "Mine got chewed up by a dog. Krista's still got her's though, right on her bed."

Lori eyed her thoughtfully. "Paige is your good friend too, isn't she?"

"Oh yeah, Paige and Julie and Krista and I hang out together all the time." Megan warmed to the subject. "Paige's cute, isn't she? Of course, she spends a lot of time on herself. She's very fussy about her clothes. Everything has to match. She always has to wear the right shoes with the right outfit. And she spends ages on her hair. But she's not conceited, not like this girl I know at camp, Erin. Erin—"

But Lori didn't want to hear about Erin. "What about Julie? What's she like?"

"Julie's a real nut," Megan said, grinning. "She gets the wildest ideas. Her father's always saying she's got a screw loose in her brain. Look, don't worry about what she said. You know, the haunted house and the ghost and all that. People say I let my imagination run wild, but she's worse!"

Sharing these thoughts about her pals with Lori was making her feel better and better. They were talking like friends! Well, at least *she* was. Lori really hadn't said much.

Megan turned to look at the clock. "Oh, the bell's about to ring. We'd better get to class." But when she turned back, Lori was already at the door. And when she got to the door, Lori was gone.

That's weird, Megan thought for at least the zillionth time since yesterday. She hurried on to class.

There were still a few minutes before the bell, and Megan decided to go over her math problems. She pulled her homework out of her notebook, and then she groaned.

"I left my math book at home," she told Krista. "Can I borrow yours for a minute?"

Krista handed it over. "Better not let Ms. Devlin know you don't have yours," she cautioned Megan. "You know how she gets when we forget our books."

Megan nodded. She opened the book and quickly went over her homework. Just as she finished, Ms. Devlin came in. "Good morning, class," she greeted them. She went to the blackboard. "Oh dear, we're out of chalk." Her eyes swept the room. "Krista, would you go to the office and get a box of chalk?"

As the teacher wrote out a hall pass for Krista, Megan took the opportunity to slip the math book back onto Krista's desk. Then she faced forward. She was determined to give the teacher her full attention today and make up for the day before.

But just as Ms. Devlin started erasing the blackboard, she heard Lori whisper her name. "Megan! Do you have a pencil I could borrow?"

Megan nodded. She opened her backpack and pulled out an extra pencil. Then she turned to hand it to Lori. She held it out toward her, but Lori was looking straight ahead.

"Lori!" she whispered.

Unfortunately, her whisper carried, and the next voice she heard was Ms. Devlin's. "What's going on back there?"

"I was just lending Lori a pencil," Megan explained.

"Lori, do you need a pencil?" the teacher asked.

Lori spoke up sweetly. "No, Ms. Devlin, I have one right here." As if to prove her point, she held up a perfectly good pencil.

Megan scratched her head. But Lori *had* asked her for a pencil.

"Megan, please face forward and don't speak to your neighbors," Ms. Devlin said.

Megan did as she was told, but she was feeling very confused. And then a strange idea hit her. Had Lori asked her for that pencil just so Megan could get caught talking? Was Lori trying to get her into trouble?

No, she told herself, that was crazy. She was doing just what Krista had accused her of, letting her imagination run wild. She must not have heard Lori properly. It was all in her head. Or maybe she should have her ears checked.

But her own arguments weren't very convincing.

The rest of the morning passed in an ordinary way, until it was time for math. "Class, open your textbooks to page twenty," Ms. Devlin said.

Megan opened her social studies book, laid her homework over it, and just hoped Ms. Devlin wouldn't call on *her* to read anything aloud from the book.

"Krista, would you read the directions, please," Ms. Devlin continued.

When there was no response, Megan glanced at Krista. She was frantically going through the books on her desk. Then she looked under her desk top.

"Krista?"

Red-faced, Krista looked up. "I'm sorry, Ms. Devlin. I can't find my book."

For once, Ms. Devlin's stern look was aimed at someone other than Megan. "Krista, you know that I require you all to be prepared."

Lori's hand shot up. "Ms. Devlin, there are two math books on my desk. I guess one of them must be Krista's. I don't know how it got here."

Neither did Megan. There was no way she had put that book on Lori's desk. She turned and watched Lori hand the book to Krista. And she didn't miss the look of distinct annoyance that

Krista shot at *her*. But there was nothing she could say about it now.

Just before lunch, Ms. Devlin told them about a special assignment. "For social studies, I'd like all of you to pair up with a classmate and choose a country that particularly interests you. You'll have two weeks to prepare a report on that country. You can concentrate on anything you like—the customs, the history, the geography, whatever! And together, each pair will present a report on that country to the class. Please spend a few moments at lunch today deciding on a partner and choosing a country."

Megan started thinking as the class rose to silently walk to the cafeteria. What country could she and Krista do? Then she remembered that Krista's father had gone to Japan on business just last year. He'd brought back tons of souvenirs, pictures, and a real kimono for Krista. They could do a great report on Japan.

Standing in the cafeteria line, waiting for her tray, she fidgeted. The line seemed incredibly slow. When she finally emerged with her tray, she headed over to her usual table. The others were already sitting there eating, which wasn't unusual. What was strange was the fact that they hadn't collected their lunch trays.

Megan was floored. Not just Krista, but Julie and Paige too had brought lunches from home.

Megan sat down and stared glumly at the gook on her tray. "I think you guys have the right idea," she sighed. "Maybe I'll start bringing my lunch too."

"Lori, you've only been here two days and you've already started a whole new trend!" Paige exclaimed.

"Megan, did you see what Lori gave Krista?" Julie asked.

Megan realized that Krista was wearing a bright, embroidered vest that she hadn't been wearing that morning. "I was admiring it in Lori's closet yesterday," Krista said. "I can't believe you're letting me have it, Lori!"

"I never wear it," Lori replied. "And it looks much better on you than on me."

"Isn't it gorgeous, Megan?" Krista asked.

Personally, Megan thought it was too flashy, but she mumbled, "Gorgeous." She wanted to tell Krista she hadn't put the textbook on Lori's desk, but she couldn't do it while Lori was there.

"What country are you guys doing for that report?" she asked Paige and Julie.

Paige looked at Julie. "You want to do Italy? My grandmother's from there, and she makes these great Italian cookies. I could get her to make some for the whole class."

"Sounds good to me," Julie replied.

Megan was just about to bring up Japan, when Lori spoke. "Krista and I are doing France."

Megan's mouth dropped open. She turned and looked at Krista in astonishment. Krista suddenly became very interested in her sandwich.

"My parents took me to France last summer," Lori went on. "And we have all these videos we took. We're going to show them in class."

What's going on here? Megan thought in bewilderment. Ever since first grade, whenever students had to pair off for anything, Krista was always her partner!

"I'm going to get some water," Lori said, and left the table. Megan took advantage of her absence to confront Krista. "I thought *we'd* be partners."

At least Krista had the courtesy to look apologetic. "She asked me to be her partner when we sat down. I felt like I had to say yes, because she really doesn't know any other students. I figured you'd understand."

Megan bit her lip. She couldn't really blame Krista. She herself would probably have done the same thing for a new student in a situation like that. But maybe she would have talked to Krista first.

Still, she couldn't make a fuss. "Okay," she sighed. "I'll find someone else."

"By the way," Krista said, "you almost got me into trouble in class! How could you put my book on Lori's desk?"

"I *didn't,*" Megan replied.

"Then how did it get there?"

"Maybe Lori took it."

Krista looked at Megan oddly. "That's silly! Why would Lori do something like that?"

Megan had no answer for that.

When Lori returned, they all started talking about a television show everyone had seen the night before. It was the kind of conversation Megan and her friends had all the time. But with Lori there, it was different. Everytime Lori spoke, she seemed to be talking to everyone but Megan.

Megan kept telling herself it was all in her head, but she couldn't help feeling uncomfortable. Finally, she rose. "I'm going to see if I can find a partner for that project," she told the others.

She went over to a table where six girls were sitting. "Does anyone need a partner for the social studies project?" she asked.

39

They all shook their heads. "Sorry," one girl said.

"That's okay," Megan murmured. The girls were looking at her oddly, and Megan wasn't surprised. Everyone knew she and Krista always worked together.

She wandered around the cafeteria, stopping every now and then to ask a classmate if she needed a partner. But everyone she spoke to already had one.

She returned to her own table. "I can't find a partner," she muttered. They were talking about something else, and no one seemed to be listening.

Megan picked up her glass of orange juice. Just as she was about to take a sip, Lori suddenly leaned to the side, jostling Megan's arm. The glass tipped, splashing juice on Krista.

"Megan!" Krista wailed, leaping up. A thin stream of orange juice trickled down her new vest.

Megan grabbed a napkin, but Krista pushed her hand away. "No, you'll only make it worse. I'm going to the rest room."

Megan went after her. "Krista, I'm sorry!"

Krista paused. She cocked her head to one side, and her eyes were slightly narrowed. "Megan . . . did you do that on purpose?"

At first, Megan was too startled to reply. Finally, she managed to say, "Of course not! Why would I do that?"

"Because Lori gave it to me."

"That's crazy!" Megan exclaimed. "It was an accident!"

Krista gazed at her, obviously unconvinced. Then she shrugged and went in the rest room.

When they got back to class, Ms. Devlin started talking about the project again. "I want to know who the teams are, and which countries you've chosen. But first, is there anyone who doesn't have a partner?"

Megan raised her hand. It was humiliating. Especially when she saw that only other hand up belonged to Jeff Tracy—the wimpiest, nerdiest dork in the entire sixth grade. He was the kind of person who was always raising his hand when the teacher asked something. Then, when he was called on, he never knew the right answer. And he told on other kids if he saw them talking in class.

Megan thought she was going to be sick when she heard Ms. Devlin's next words. "Megan and Jeff can work together then. Do you know which country you'd like?"

Megan's knowledge of geography seemed to evaporate. She couldn't think of any place in the world. And Jeff just stared at Ms. Devlin dumbly.

"Well, let's see what the other students have chosen first," Ms. Devlin said. She went through the class, identifying the teams and noting the countries they picked. When she finished, she studied her list. "Let's see, no one's doing Holland. Megan and Jeff, why don't you do your report on Holland."

Megan nodded glumly. Holland was probably a perfectly nice country. But she'd most likely end up hating it after having to study it with Jeff.

"I'll be giving you some class time to work on this," Ms. Devlin told them. "But I expect you to spend time outside of class too."

Megan moaned slightly. Spend time outside of class with Jeff Tracy? The mere thought made her stomach turn over. Krista should feel especially bad now about abandoning Megan for this project.

As soon as the bell rang at the end of the school day, Jeff bounded over to her seat. "We should go to the library."

Megan gazed at him in horror. "Now?"

He nodded. "Then we won't have to meet anymore to work on it. We can divide up the topics and work on our own."

42

He didn't seem to be any more thrilled about their working together than she was. That was fine with Megan. And maybe she should go ahead and meet with him today. At least it would get that part over with.

"Okay," she relented. Jeff went back to his seat to get his stuff. Megan got up and went over to Paige's desk, where Julie, Krista, and Lori were gathered. She looked at Krista's vest.

"Oh good, the stain came out."

"Yeah," Krista said. She still appeared a little disgruntled, though.

"Poor Megan." Julie sighed. "I'm sorry you got stuck with Jeff."

Paige wore the same expression of sympathy. Krista looked sorry too, but not as guilty as Megan thought she'd be. Only Lori didn't appear to care about Megan's misfortune.

"He wants to go to the library now," Megan told them. "I figured I might as well get that over with."

"Oh, no!" Paige exclaimed. "Lori just said if we go over to her place, her mother will drive us to the new bowling alley!"

Megan winced. She'd been dying to go there. "I'll get out of this meeting with Jeff," she told the girls.

"Don't bother," Lori said. "I feel awful about

this, but my mother's car only holds four passengers." She talked as if she was really, truly sorry. But her back was to the others as she spoke to Megan, and only Megan could see the smile of satisfaction on her face.

No, this was definitely not all in her head.

Chapter 4

Cold cereal wasn't exactly Megan's favorite breakfast. But it didn't matter that next morning. Like a robot, she spooned the flakes into her mouth without even tasting them.

"Megan, is something wrong?"

Lost in her thoughts, her father's voice startled her. Hastily, she swallowed. "Huh? Oh, no, nothing's wrong." She didn't feel like talking about Lori, not to her dad. Although he was usually pretty sensitive about her various problems, she doubted that he'd be able to understand this one. Not when she didn't even understand it herself.

But as his searching eyes remained on her, she had to say something. "I was just thinking about this social studies project. Do you know anything about Holland?"

45

"Tulips and windmills," Mr. Lindsay replied promptly. "That's all, I'm afraid."

Her mother breezed into the kitchen. "I've got to run," she said. She'd just recently started back to work part-time, and still tended to be a little frazzled and distracted in the mornings on the days she worked. She scooped Alex out of his high chair. "I'll drop this little fellow off at the day-care center." She glanced at the clock. "Megan!"

"Yeah, Mom?"

"Look at the time! Hasn't Krista come by yet?"

Megan jumped up. "Oh no!" Hastily, she wiped her mouth. "Gee, Krista's never been late before. She must be sick or something."

"But she would have called, wouldn't she?" her mother asked.

Megan was in too much of a rush to consider this. She gathered her stuff, ran out of the house, and dashed next door. "Krista! Krista!"

A second later, the door opened and Krista's mother stuck her head out. "Krista left for school a while ago, Megan."

Megan was dumbfounded. "Why didn't she come by for me?"

Krista's mother looked just as puzzled as Megan. "I have no idea, dear."

46

Megan couldn't afford to spend any more time questioning her. She sped down the street.

But running as fast as she could wasn't much help. As she tore into the school building, panting and out of breath, the deserted hallway was a bad sign. When she saw the clock in the hallway, she wanted to cry. She was ten minutes late. And there was no point in hoping that Ms. Devlin wouldn't be in the room twice in one month.

She opened the classroom door and entered, with a weak, regretful smile. That did nothing to effect the stern face Ms. Devlin turned to her. "Megan, do you have a note?"

"No, Ms. Devlin."

"Then that's fifteen minutes detention."

It was what Megan expected. Glumly, she nodded. Her face was flushed as she moved down the aisle toward her desk. Embarrassed, she tried not to look directly at her classmates, but she sensed the sympathy in most of their faces. There was one major exception, however. Lori was definitely smirking.

Megan was more interested in someone else. She tried to catch Krista's eye. She didn't dare speak, but her expression clearly asked "what happened?"

47

But Krista didn't see the question. She stared straight ahead.

Throughout the morning, Megan sneaked peeks at her best friend. She couldn't imagine what had prevented Krista from calling for her. Her mind concocted possible explanations. Maybe Krista *had* come by, but Megan hadn't heard her. She might have called and called, and then got frustrated when Megan didn't come out. Maybe she stalked off to school in anger.

It was a good story, but not easy to believe. If that was what happened, why didn't Krista simply ring the door bell? It just didn't make sense. For five years they'd been walking to school together. Why was today different?

Megan was finding it very hard to concentrate on the teacher. She *had* to know what was going on. And she couldn't wait till lunchtime to find out.

Tearing a sheet of paper out of her binder, she scrawled a note. *Why didn't you come by for me this morning?* She folded the paper, and watched Ms. Devlin.

As soon as the teacher turned her back on the class to write on the blackboard, she hissed "Krista!" Then she leaned to the side and extended the note.

From behind Krista, Lori reached out and snatched it. At first, Megan thought she was just going to pass it on to Krista. To her horror, Lori began opening the note. And she didn't even do it under her desk. She held it right up in front of her.

Ms. Devlin turned back to the class. "Lori, what have you got there?"

"I don't know, Ms. Devlin. Megan passed me this note."

Ms. Devlin frowned. "Megan, you know my policy on passing notes. Now, I won't embarrass you by asking you to read it in front of the class. Lori, throw the note away." As Lori got up and pranced over to the wastebasket, Ms. Devlin continued. "Since you're new here, Lori, I'll let it go this time. But in the future, don't accept any notes offered to you. Megan, you should know better. I'm afraid that's an additional fifteen minutes detention."

Megan slumped down in her seat.

She wished she'd brought her lunch. Then she wouldn't have to wait and wait in this stupid line for food she didn't even want to eat. And not just because it was crummy food. The cafeteria could be offering Big Macs with french fries, and she still wouldn't be able to eat. Something was very, very wrong, and her stomach was tied up in knots.

Finally, she got her tray and hurried toward her usual table. Then she stopped short. The table was empty. She looked around the noisy, crowded cafeteria, and spotted them—Krista, Paige, Julie, and Lori. They were at one of the smaller tables, one with only four chairs.

Slowly, Megan made her way there. She stood there awkwardly, balancing her tray and waiting for someone to say something. But no one did.

"Krista?"

With a great show of reluctance, Krista turned to her. The look on her face made Megan take a step backward. She knew that look. She'd seen Krista direct it toward her kid brother when he messed around with her stuff, at Jeff Tracy when he tattled on someone in class, at a nasty neighbor who made a fuss when Krista's dog entered her yard. The look meant she was furious. Megan had seen it before, but never aimed in *her* direction.

She realized that Paige and Julie were wearing equally hostile expressions. "What's going on?" she asked. "Why are we sitting here?" She started to place her tray on the table, and Krista spoke.

"There's no room here, Megan."

In total bewilderment, Megan stared at her friends. "Is this a joke or something?"

"It's no joke," Lori said smoothly. "You'll have to find another place to sit."

Megan had never been punched in the stomach but she had a notion this must be how it felt. Feeling dizzy and confused, she made her way over to an empty table and sat down. But she kept her eyes on the girls. When Krista got up and went into the rest room, Megan waited a few minutes, debating with herself. Then, with determination, she rose and followed her.

Krista was washing her hands at the sink when Megan walked in. Luckily, they were alone in the rest room. "Krista, what's going on?" Megan burst out. "Why are you acting like this? Why didn't you come by for me this morning?"

Krista's eyes were blazing. "Oh, Megan, don't be dense! Did you honestly think we wouldn't find out?"

"Find out what?"

"What you told Lori about us! It's incredible! How could you do such a thing?"

Utterly perplexed, Megan stared at her. "I don't know what you're talking about!"

"Sure you don't," Krista snorted. "You don't

remember telling Lori that Paige doesn't care about anything except how she looks. And Julie's a dippy space cadet. And that I . . . that I sleep with a teddy bear!"

Megan couldn't be sure she'd heard correctly. Her head was spinning. "But—that's not—I didn't—"

Krista wouldn't let her continue. "Don't try to lie and blame it on poor Lori. *Someone* had to tell her that stuff about us. Now I understand why Lori doesn't like you. And you can add me and Paige and Julie to the list of people who don't like you either." She pulled a paper towel from the dispenser, dried her hands, and marched out.

Megan didn't feel like she'd been punched in the stomach anymore. Now she felt like she'd been kicked in the head.

Chapter 5

At noon on Saturday, Megan stood in front of the community center and looked for her mother's car. She shifted her tennis racket from one arm to the other. It felt like it weighed a ton. It had been feeling like that all morning.

As she waited, she saw the teenaged girl she'd played with come out of the center. She gave her a halfhearted wave and called, "Congratulations."

"Thanks," the girl said. "You know, I've seen you play before. I never would have thought I could beat you."

Neither would I, Megan replied silently. But she just shrugged and smiled thinly.

"I guess you were off your game today," the older girl continued. "Lucky for me!"

I've certainly made her happy, Megan

thought. At least something good has come out of my misery.

Megan watched her walk away. She didn't even know the girl's name. She'd seen her hanging around the court this morning, looking like she needed a partner. In the first few minutes of the game, Megan could see that she was just a beginner at tennis. It didn't matter. A toddler could have beaten Megan today. If there was one thing Megan knew for sure about her tennis skill, it was the fact that her tennis playing was always affected by her mood. And she couldn't remember ever having been in such a bad one.

She spotted her mother's car coming into the circular driveway and walked over to meet it.

"Hi, honey," her mother said as she climbed in. "Good game today?"

"So-so," Megan replied. Mrs. Lindsay took a quick sideways glance at her before giving her full attention to the road ahead. Her mother had always been pretty good at detecting when something was wrong.

And Megan knew that there was one major clue—the fact that she'd been very quiet for the past couple of days. Which wasn't like her at all.

But her mother didn't say anything or ask any questions. Megan liked the fact that her mother never nagged her to reveal a problem. She waited for Megan to come to her. And Megan just wasn't ready to talk about this situation yet.

"I have to stop at the market before I drop you at the mall," her mother mentioned.

"I'm not going to the mall," Megan said. "I just want to go home."

It was a good thing her mother had to concentrate on her driving, or Megan would have received one long searching look. Instead, there was a long silence, and then a quiet, "All right, Megan."

As soon as they got home, Megan went directly to her room. Piled on her desk were books about Holland from the library. But she wasn't in the mood to work on the report. She tried to think of something else, anything else, that would take her mind off her problems.

Her eyes lit on the letter she'd received over a week ago from Sarah. She still hadn't responded to it. She sat down at her desk and took a sheet of blue stationery from the drawer.

She started the letter in her usual way. *Dear Sarah, How are you? I'm* . . . Then she stopped and put down her pen. She couldn't write *I'm fine,* like she always did. Because she wasn't fine. Megan always had a hard time lying to people face-to-face. It was just as difficult writing a lie.

Maybe writing about it all would help. With a sigh, she picked up her pen.

I'm not fine. Everything's been going wrong. There's a new girl at school named Lori. I beat her in a tennis tournament last spring, and I guess she hates me for that. She's ruining my life. She told lies to all my friends and made them mad at me. Now no one's speaking to me. And that's not all. Because of Lori, I keep getting into trouble at school. She got my friend Krista to work with her on a report, so I got stuck working with the biggest creep in class. Yesterday at school, we were choosing sides for a volleyball game. Lori was captain of one side and Krista was captain of the other. Neither of them would choose me. I've never been the last person left to be picked for team! Even Jeff Tracy (the creep) got picked before me! I can't concentrate on tennis, and today I lost a game to a girl who doesn't even know how to play! Everything is terrible.

Her hand was aching from gripping the pen too hard. She put it down again. Writing the letter wasn't helping at all. If anything, it was making her feel worse.

She opened one of the books on her desk and began reading.

Holland is well-known for its beautiful fields of tulips. Bulb-growing is a Dutch specialty. The first tulips were brought to Holland from Turkey in 1559.

She closed the book. Who cared about tulips and what happened in 1559? Then she yawned. Funny, she never got sleepy in the middle of the afternoon. She decided to do something she hadn't done since she was a little kid—take a nap. At least if she was sleeping, she wouldn't be able to think. She lay down on her bed and closed her eyes.

When she next opened them, she was amazed to realize she actually had slept. Outside, the sun was going down. She checked the clock, and saw that it was just after five o'clock. Another hour and a half to kill before dinner.

She went to her desk and pulled out her photo scrapbook. Opening it, she looked at the photos from last summer. Her eyes began stinging as she examined the faces of Trina, Sarah, Katie, and Erin, her Sunnyside cabin mates. *They* never got mad at her. Okay, maybe once in a while someone would yell at her about something she had done. But they'd never stopped speaking to her.

Turning a few pages, she came across a photo of Krista and herself. Each had one arm slung over the other's shoulder. She remembered the occasion. It was Krista's tenth birthday, and Megan had gone to her house for a sleepover.

Next to that picture was one of Megan, Krista, Paige, and Julie in the middle of a pillow fight. Looking at it, she could almost hear the giggles and shrieks.

The stinging in her eyes got worse. And then she felt something wet on her cheeks.

"Megan!"

Hastily, Megan wiped her eyes. Without looking in the mirror, she knew that her eyes would be red and puffy and that her mother would be able to tell what Megan had just been doing. Sure enough, when her mother came into the bedroom, she gazed at Megan in concern. She seemed to be on the verge of giving in and demanding that Megan tell her what the problem was. But instead, she bit her lip, and then smiled brightly.

"I'm going over to the church. They're having a fund-raising sale today, things people have donated, and a bake sale too. Want to come with me?"

Anything was better than sitting around and moping. "Okay, Mom."

"You can help me pick out a cake for dessert tonight," her mother added. "Um, you might want to wash your face first."

Megan went to the bathroom and splashed some cold water on her face. Her eyes still looked red. She went back to her room and fumbled in a drawer until she found some sunglasses and put them on.

When her mother saw her, her eyebrows went up. Her mouth opened, and then snapped shut. Megan knew she was about to ask why she was wearing sunglasses when the sun had gone down, but had thought better of it. "I'll meet you in the car," Megan said, and went outside through the back door, in order not to run into her father who was watching a football game in the living room. He might not be quite as tactful as her mother.

When they arrived at the church, the sight of all the people coming and going cheered Megan slightly. And when she saw all the interesting things laid out on tables inside, she brightened. This might actually be fun, she thought.

"I'm going to look at these antiques for a moment," Mrs. Lindsay told her. "Why don't you go check out the cakes and see if there's anything that looks particularly scrumptious."

Megan went over to a long table where cakes, pies, cookies, and other assorted goodies were displayed. Talk about scrumptious. This wasn't going to be an easy decision.

She was debating the merits of carrot cake over chocolate mocha when she heard a familiar and not very welcome voice coming from a table behind her.

"There's a place that rents costumes over by the new bowling alley," Lori was saying. "I think we should all wear something really wild and unusual. We don't want to be ordinary ghosts and witches."

Megan stiffened as she heard Krista's reply. "Absolutely! This is going to be so much fun. I've never been to a real Halloween party."

"I can't believe your parents are letting you invite all the girls in class." That was Julie's voice.

Lori giggled. "All but one, of course."

Then Megan heard Paige, talking more quietly. "Speaking of that one . . ." Her voice trailed off. Megan knew they'd spotted her. She heard Lori giggle again.

"Can you believe those sunglasses? Who does she think she is, a movie star?"

It was all Megan could do to keep from picking up a pie, whirling around, and throwing it directly into one of their faces. Or maybe pick up four pies and hit all of them. Clenching her fists, and keeping her back to them, she edged away.

She had to get out of there. She grabbed the closest cake, not even caring what it was, and headed toward her mother. "Here, Mom."

Her mother looked puzzled. "I thought you didn't like coconut."

"I like it now," Megan said quickly. "Um, I'm going outside, okay?"

Without waiting for a reply, she hurried out of the church. Sticking her hands in her jeans pockets, she ambled down the sidewalk. She didn't care what Lori said, she was glad she was wearing the sunglasses. No one could see that she was crying again.

Then she saw something out of the corner of her eye. She looked up.

She was standing right in front of that old, run-down house. Suddenly, she could feel her heart beating harder than normal. Was she seeing things now?

She took off the sunglasses. Then she practically choked. Up on the second floor, a light was shining through a window. And in that window she could clearly see the shadow of a woman.

Megan blinked. Then she rubbed her eyes. The light and the woman were still there.

Frantically, she looked around for someone to show this to. She spotted her mother coming out of the church. "Mom!" she shouted. "Mom, come here!"

Her arms laden with packages, Mrs. Lindsay ran over. "Megan, what's the matter?"

"Mom, look!" Megan pointed.

"Look at what?"

The window was dark. Megan gazed up and shook her head in wonderment. Could she have just been imaging it?

"What did you see, Megan?"

Megan sighed. "Nothing. I mean, I thought I saw something, but . . . it's not there."

Her mother smiled. "Daydreaming again, right?"

"Yeah, I guess. Here, I'll carry some of those things." Together, they went back to the car.

"I saw your friends in there," Mrs. Lindsay said. "Krista, and Julie, and . . . Megan! Sweetie, what's wrong?"

She'd forgotten to put her sunglasses back on.

And the tears were streaming down on her face. "Oh, Mom . . . Mom, everything's just awful!"

Her mother had just put the key into the ignition, but she didn't start the car. She put her arm around Megan, and let her cry.

When there were no tears left, Megan told her the whole story. "No one's speaking to me, Mom. Not even Krista! She wouldn't even listen to me when I tried to tell her it was all lies, what Lori said. What am I going to do?"

Her mother stroked her hair. "Maybe you'd just better ignore it for a while. If this Lori is as unkind as you say, Krista and the others are bound to figure that out sooner or later. Then they'll listen to you, and you'll all make up."

Megan sniffed. "What am I going to do in the meantime? Lori's having a Halloween party, and she's inviting all the girls in class except me!"

Mrs. Lindsay was silent for a minute. Then she said, "Why don't you have your own Halloween party?"

"My own Halloween party?" Megan rolled her eyes. "It wouldn't be much of a party. I don't have any friends to invite to it."

"I wouldn't say that."

Megan looked at her curiously. Her mother's eyes were sparkling.

"Who do you think I could invite?"

Mrs. Lindsay smiled. "How about your Sunnyside friends?"

Chapter 6

Six days later, on Friday morning, Megan woke up happy for the first time in ages. It wasn't the memory of the past week that made her smile. That week had been just as bad as the week before. Maybe worse. Lori had invited all the other girls in the class to her Halloween party. And she'd made it very clear why she was leaving Megan out. Now everyone was giving her funny looks, and Megan was eating lunch all alone.

Then there was the stupid social studies assignment. Three times that week Ms. Devlin had sent the class to the library to work on their reports. Three times, Megan had been forced to sit with creepy Jeff, looking at each other's notes on Holland and organizing their report. A couple of boys had actually teased her about spending so much time with him. As if she liked him!

And to top everything off, she was now on Ms. Devlin's bad side. The teacher wouldn't take her eyes off Megan, as she watched for any signs of daydreaming.

But today, Megan wasn't going to think about any of those bad things in her life. She still had friends, even if none of them lived right here in town. And those friends were coming to visit today.

There was a light knock on her door. "Megan?"

"C'mon in, Mom."

Her mother entered and gazed at her reprovingly. "Isn't it time you got out of bed?"

Megan stretched. "But there's no school today, Mom!" She sat up. "Wasn't that incredible good luck? A state teachers' meeting the day before Halloween! Now I get three days with my buddies instead of just two!"

"And they're all going to be here around noon," Mrs. Lindsay noted. "Which is why I suggest you get up."

Megan twisted her head to eye the clock on her nightstand. "It's only eight-thirty. I've got at least two hours."

Her mother nodded. "And you've got at least two hours of cleaning and straightening up to do in this room."

Megan looked around. Her mother had a point. "Okay," she relented. She swung her legs over the side of the bed. "I'll get right to work." Jumping off the bed, she began snatching up clothes from the floor.

Mrs. Lindsay laughed. "I think there will be plenty of time after you get dressed and have some breakfast."

The next couple of hours flew by. Just before noon, Megan was in the kitchen, helping her mother prepare a huge amount of tuna salad when they heard a honking car pull into the driveway. With a shriek of joy, Megan ran outside.

If possible, Katie's shriek was even louder. The two girls ran into each other's arms, where they hugged and jumped up and down together.

"I can't believe I'm here!" Katie screeched. "Am I the first?"

"Yeah," Megan said. Then, peering down the road, she added, "but not for long."

A black limousine was pulling up in front of the house. Only one person Megan knew would arrive anywhere in a car like that. The girls raced down the lawn.

A uniformed man opened the back door of the limousine, and Erin stepped out. When she saw Megan and Katie, she too started to shriek, and then clapped a hand to her mouth. Shrieks weren't Erin's style. And neither were hugs.

"Honestly, you guys," she muttered as Megan and Katie practically jumped on her. But her words couldn't prevent a look of pleasure from appearing on her face. When the girls released her, she smoothed the wrinkles they'd made in her jacket. "You're both such children."

Katie chortled. "What do you think we should do, shake hands?"

"We could start greeting each other the way French people do," Erin suggested. "My mother showed me how when she got back from Europe. Watch."

She leaned toward Megan, kissed one of her cheeks and then the other. Actually, they weren't really kisses—it was more like brushing cheeks. But Megan made a point of rubbing her cheek vigorously, and saying, "Yuck! Gross!"

Meanwhile, Katie was still jumping up and down. "This is so great! A Sunnyside Halloween! And wait'll you guys see my costume!"

"Costume!" Erin rolled her eyes. "I hope we're not going to trick-or-treat. We're too old for that. At least, *I* am."

Her wrinkled nose and look of disdain didn't bother Megan at all. She could always rely on

Erin to put the others' ideas down. But in the end, she always came around.

Mrs. Lindsay called from the door. "Girls, why don't you come inside?"

But just as they started toward the house, another car slowed to a stop. This time, shrieks escalated to screams as Sarah and Trina emerged from the car. Within seconds, they all congregated in a big group hug.

"I'm so happy we're all here together," Megan squealed. She felt like laughing and crying at the same time.

"It's like old times," Sarah exclaimed. "I've missed you all so much!" In Megan's ear, she whispered, "Especially you."

"Really, girls," Erin said in her most adult voice. "It's only been two months."

"Feels like two years to me," Megan murmured.

"Well, we're all here now," Trina stated.

"Sunnyside forever!" Katie shouted.

"Could we *please* go inside?" Erin asked. "I don't know about the rest of you, but *I'd* like to freshen up."

Carrying suitcases, they all headed toward the house, with everyone talking at once. "Why didn't you answer my last letter?" Sarah asked Megan.

Megan lowered her voice. "I started to, but it was too depressing." When Sarah gazed at her in concern, she added, "I'll tell you about it later."

"I'm getting lunch ready," Mrs. Lindsay announced to the girls when they came inside.

"Can we help you?" Trina asked.

"No, dear, why don't you go on to Megan's room and relax. I'm sure you've got a lot to catch up on."

Megan led them to her room, where they all settled on her twin beds.

"How come you guys came together?" Katie asked Sarah and Trina.

"My mother was visiting Dr. Fine today," Trina told them. "So I went with her, and then Sarah's sister drove us here."

Erin looked at them with interest. "Why was your mother visiting Sarah's father?"

"Well, you know my mother wrote that magazine article about Dr. Fine's medical research," Trina replied. "Then we all ran into each other at a carnival, and they started talking. Anyway, they got to be friends and they get together sometimes." She was blushing slightly as she said this.

Sarah broke in. "They're just good friends. So don't get any ideas, Megan!"

Megan laughed. She remembered when Sarah's father and Trina's mother met during a visit to their daughters at Sunnyside. They spent a lot of time together, and everyone got the idea something romantic was going on between them.

"It's nice for us," Sarah went on. "Now I get to see Trina more. And it's great talking to Mrs. Sandburg. She gives me advice on my writing."

"Dr. Fine's really neat," Trina added. "He took us bird-watching. And he taught me how to do bird calls. Listen!" She took a deep breath. Then, out of her mouth, came these loud honking sounds. Everyone cracked up.

"Do the owl," Sarah urged her. Trina obliged. It was wild! Megan had never heard a real owl before, but she could have sworn there was one right there in the bedroom.

"Katie, what's your news?" Megan asked.

"School's great this year. I was elected president of the sixth grade. We're working on an antidrug campaign, and I've been trying to organize a fair to raise money for homeless people."

Trina nodded with approval. "That sounds good."

"I wish I could get everyone to feel that way,"

Katie said. "It's hard to get kids involved. But I'm winning them over."

Megan looked at her in admiration. Katie could handle just about anything. *She'd* never let other kids gang up on her.

"Sarah, what are you up to?" Katie asked.

"Well, there's a big essay contest at school. And my teacher thinks I can win." She smiled happily. "I've got a wonderful teacher this year. She's so understanding! Once, she caught me reading a paperback during math. I had it tucked inside my textbook. And she wasn't even angry!"

Megan was envious. Sarah's teacher certainly sounded a lot different from Ms. Devlin.

"Well, *I've* got some big news," Erin announced. She paused dramatically until she was sure she had everyone's attention. "My parents want to send me to Europe this spring, over the spring break."

The other cabin six girls looked suitably impressed. "Well, if you go to Holland, I can tell you all about it," Megan said, sighing. "I'm working on a social studies report. With the creepiest boy in class for a partner."

"How come you're not working with one of your friends?" Katie asked.

Megan bit her lip. Hastily, she changed the subject. "What else is new, Erin?"

"I took a class at a department store on using makeup," she reported. "Of course, my parents still won't let me wear makeup to school. But at least I'll know how to use it properly when they let me."

"Maybe you could put makeup on us for Halloween," Katie suggested. "Megan, what are we going to do for Halloween, anyway?"

Megan thought. "Well, we could dress up and go around the neighborhood. I know it's a little babyish," she added quickly, before Erin could object. "But I know some neighbors who give out really great stuff. And we could pick up some really scary movies at the video store for later on."

Trina smiled. "Remember when scary movies used to freak you out?"

"But I haven't had nightmares in ages," Megan said proudly.

"Are your friends going to hang out with us?" Sarah asked.

Megan swallowed. "My friends?"

"Yeah," Katie said. "The kids you're always telling us about. Krista, and Julie, and—who's the other one?"

"Paige," Megan replied automatically. "No, they won't be hanging out with us."

There must have been something sad in the way she said that. Four curious pairs of eyes were focused on her. Katie, as usual, was blunt. "Why not?"

Megan hesitated. She'd planned to tell only Sarah, when they could get a minute alone. But she couldn't keep a secret from these guys.

"It all started when this new girl, Lori, came to school two weeks ago." As she told her story, she had their full attention. And when she finished, Sarah put an arm around her. "Oh, Megan. That's really crummy."

"Truly terrible," Trina said softly, her eyes warm with compassion.

Erin shuddered. "It must be awful for you. Of course, I don't know what it's like to be unpopular, but it can't be much fun."

"It's an outrage!" Katie stated fiercely. "And you shouldn't stand for it! Don't let people treat you like that, Megan!"

"What can I do about it?" Megan asked.

Katie frowned. "I don't know yet. But I'll think of something."

"She will, too," Sarah affirmed. "Like the time Carolyn had to leave camp for a while. Remember the way she figured out how we could get rid of those awful substitute counselors?"

Megan's eyes lit up. "That's right!" She grinned at Katie. "You always have brilliant ideas."

"Not *always*," Erin said. "I can think of one or two of her brilliant schemes that didn't exactly work."

So could Megan. But right now, she'd hold on to anything that might help. "I'll try any scheme that Katie can come up with," she said stoutly. "Even if it flops, I can't be any worse off than I am now."

"Girls!" Mrs. Lindsay's voice rang out. "Lunch is served!"

The cabin mates hurried to the kitchen, where Mrs. Lindsay had laid out a great spread. Little Alex bounced up and down in his high chair at the sight of all these strangers. Trina immediately started playing peekaboo with him, while the others filled their plates.

They didn't talk about Megan's problem over lunch, which was fine with her. This was her weekend to forget all about it. Instead, they talked about camp, reliving their adventures and experiences—at least, the ones they could talk about in front of Megan's mother!

75

"What are your plans for this afternoon?" Mrs. Lindsay asked them.

"I thought we'd all go to the bowling alley," Megan said.

"All right!" Katie cheered. "I've been bowling a lot lately. I'm going to blow you guys away!"

"Bowling?" Erin's expression made it clear what she thought of that idea.

"We have a brand-new bowling alley in town," Megan told them. "I haven't been there yet, but everyone says it's very cool."

"Cool? A bowling alley?" Erin's eyebrows reached her hairline.

"I like bowling," Trina mused. "But I'd never describe it as 'cool.' "

But when they entered the new bowling alley, Trina had to admit she'd never seen a bowling alley like this before. There was the usual line of lanes, each ending in a set of pins. But the walls were decorated with neon graffiti, rock music was blaring, and there was a cute little café over to the side. Even the shoes they traded their own in for weren't the usual bowling shoes—they were gold and silver and they glittered.

"Wow, this *is* cool," Katie said.

Erin was impressed too. "If all bowling alleys were like this, I could get into it."

"Have you ever played before?" Sarah asked her.

"No," Erin replied. "But I've seen people play. You just roll the bowl down the lane toward the pins, right?"

"I think there's a little more to it than that," Trina said.

Erin shrugged. "How hard could it be to knock those pins down?"

Katie winked at Megan. "Oh, not hard at all, Erin."

They found an empty lane and selected their balls. Trina went first. She got three pins down on her first throw, and two more on the next.

"Not bad," Katie said kindly as she marked the score.

Megan went next. She hit all but three pins on her first attempt, but didn't get any more on her next try.

"Better luck next time," Katie said as Sarah went up for her turn. Her toss was totally off, and the ball went directly into the gutter. Sarah, who was accustomed to not doing so well in sports, just gave a good-natured shrug.

"Okay, big shot, it's your turn," Trina said to Katie.

Katie strutted over to the lane and lifted her ball. She glanced over her shoulder at the others. "Now, watch a pro!" She took aim, and tossed the ball. Only two pins went down.

"That was just practice," she said. The ball returned, and she went for her second throw. Once again, she hit two pins.

"I just need to warm up," she told the others. "Erin, it's your turn." As Erin went to get the ball, Katie grinned wickedly. "This ought to be good for a laugh."

Erin didn't even aim. She strolled over the lane and threw the ball. Straight and fast, it headed down the center of the lane.

"Erin!" Megan shrieked. "You got a strike!"

Erin smiled casually. "See? I told you it was easy."

"Beginner's luck," Katie growled.

But as the game progressed, it appeared that Erin had a natural talent for bowling. Once Katie's initial dismay wore off, she accepted this good-naturedly, and just took it as a challenge. The girls got sillier and sillier. Megan was giggling and fooling around, and feeling like her old self again. When her turn came around next, she got eight pins down.

"Hey, I'm going to get a spare," she announced. When the ball came back, she made a big show of posing before the lane and aiming.

"Come on, Megan, throw it!" Katie yelled.

Megan swung back the arm holding the ball. As she did, she turned her head. And then she froze. Entering the lane right next to them were Krista, Julie, Paige, and Lori.

Megan dropped the ball. She didn't even notice when it swerved into the gutter.

Chapter 7

With her eyes firmly set straight ahead, Megan went back to her friends.

"What happened to you?" Katie asked. "You could have made that spare."

Megan smiled thinly and sat awkwardly in a position where her back would be to the girls in the next lane. Erin went to take her turn.

Sarah edged closer to Megan and spoke in an undertone. "Why do those girls next to us keep looking at you? Do you know any of them?"

"Sort of," Megan admitted in a whisper. "Those are the girls I was telling you about. Krista, Paige, Julie, and Lori."

Before Megan could stop her, Sarah beckoned Katie and Trina over and reported what Megan had told her. Trina took a furtive peek at them.

"Gee, they *look* like nice girls."

"Appearances are deceiving," Katie stated

firmly. She grimaced. "I feel like going right over there and telling them a thing or two."

Megan shook her head. "Don't do that," she pleaded. "I don't to want to make a fuss. Just ignore them, okay?"

"You can't ignore your problems," Katie told her. "If you want to solve this, you have to confront them."

Resolutely, Megan shook her head again. "Not now. I want to forget all about them for this weekend, at least."

Katie's expression made her disapproval clear, but Megan knew she wouldn't do anything that was completely against Megan's request.

But she herself couldn't resist a quick glance at the girls in the next lane. At least they weren't looking at her or whispering and giggling. In fact, they didn't even look as if they were having a particularly good time.

Erin returned. "Hey, you didn't put down my score," she accused Katie. "I got another strike."

"Okay," Katie said, and made a notation on the scoring sheet.

Erin frowned. "You weren't even watching me. What were you guys talking about?"

"Oh, nothing," Megan said quickly. "Whose turn is it?"

Megan tried hard to keep on enjoying herself. But it wasn't easy with her former friends and her number-one enemy so close. She wanted to concentrate on the game, but her next two balls went straight into the gutter.

"Megan, what's the matter with you?" Katie asked. "I know you can play better than that."

Trina understood. "It must feel creepy, with those girls right there."

"Don't let them ruin your game," Sarah said.

Why not? Megan wondered. They're ruining my life. But she changed the subject. "Where's Erin?"

"She went to get something to drink," Trina said.

Megan sat down to watch Sarah make another attempt to hit a pin or two. But once again, her eyes strayed to the next lane. Paige was throwing the bowling ball. Whenever they all used to play at the old bowling alley, Paige always won. But watching her, Megan thought her game was off today.

Cautiously, she examined the others. Julie didn't seem like her usual self. She was slumped in her seat, twisting a lock of hair. Krista was sitting there too, just staring into space. She couldn't see Lori.

Krista turned her head abruptly and met Megan's eyes. Very quickly, they both looked away.

Sarah returned and sat close to Megan. "Do you want to leave?"

She did. But she shook her head. She wasn't going to let them drive her away.

From behind them, Megan heard Erin's tinkling laugh, and then her voice. "I know exactly what you mean! If she just cut her hair, she'd be really cute."

Who was Erin talking to? Megan wondered. And who was she talking about? She shifted around.

Her eyes widened and her mouth fell open. There stood Erin and Lori, together, talking like old friends.

"I have to show you my costume," Lori was saying. "It's so adorable!"

By now, Sarah, Trina, and Katie had spotted them too. They hurried over to Megan. "What's Erin doing?" Sarah asked.

"I have no idea," Megan murmured.

They all watched as Erin followed Lori to the lane next to them. Lori opened a bag and held up a silvery dress covered in glitter.

"What are you going to be?" Erin asked.

"A rock star!" Lori reached back into the bag. "See, it comes with this wild pink wig and a mask."

"That's fantastic," Erin gushed. "Where did you get all this stuff?"

"I rented it at the costume store. It's just a block down from here."

Watching and listening, Megan felt sick. How could Erin be so chummy with that girl? Then she remembered that Erin hadn't been listening when Megan had pointed them out. She'd just have to wait until Erin returned to tell her to stay away from them.

But Katie wasn't so patient. "Erin!"

Erin looked up. "What?"

"Katie, *don't,*" Megan hissed. She didn't want World War Three breaking out in a bowling alley.

But fortunately, Katie remembered Megan's plea. "Erin, it's your turn."

Then, right before Megan's horrified eyes, Erin turned to Lori and said, "Come on over and meet my friends." A sly smile appeared on Lori's face, and she actually accompanied Erin.

Erin appeared to be totally oblivious of the uncomfortable faces of her cabin mates. Her tone was bubbly as she made introductions.

"Everyone, this is Lori. Lori, that's Katie, Trina, Sarah, and Megan."

"Erin . . ." Megan began urgently, but Erin continued to prattle.

"Guess what? This is such a coincidence! We were both at the soda counter, and I just *knew* I had seen her before. I kept looking at her, and she kept looking at me, and then I remembered! Lori's cousin is a neighbor of mine back home! And I met Lori last year when she was visiting her cousin. Isn't that absolutely amazing!"

"Amazing," Katie repeated grimly.

"Erin . . ." This time Megan put more desperation in her voice, but Erin still didn't pick up on her tone.

"And listen to this! Lori's having a big Halloween party tomorrow night, and she invited—"

"Erin!" Megan cried in despair.

Erin stopped. "What?"

"Excuse me," Lori said sweetly. "But I think it's my turn. It was nice to meet you. *Most* of you." She scampered back to her own lane.

Erin's brow puckered slightly as she gazed after her. "What did she mean by that?"

"Oh, *Erin,*" Sarah moaned.

"What's wrong?" Erin asked.

Megan motioned for her to come closer. "Erin, that's the girl I told you about. The new girl who hates me and who's been getting me into trouble and lying to my friends about me so they'd hate me too."

"The one who's making Megan's life miserable," Katie added for emphasis.

Erin was clearly shocked. "You're kidding! Lori Landers? But she's cool! I like her!"

Katie spoke through gritted teeth. "Erin, how can you say that after what she's done to Megan?"

"I didn't know till now, did I?" Erin retorted. She patted Megan's shoulder. "Sorry."

"Well, you know now," Sarah said. "So I hope you're not planning to become buddies with her. There's such a thing as cabin six loyalty, even when we're not at Sunnyside."

"Okay, okay," Erin replied.

"Erin!"

All the girls turned. Lori was leaning over the ledge that separated the two lanes. "I just wanted to tell you, I meant that about my party. I'd love for you to come. And bring your friends. *Some* of them."

Megan stared at her stonily. Then she turned to see Erin's reaction.

Erin was biting her lip. Then, with an

abashed smile, she said, "Gee, I wish I could, but . . ."

Katie took over. "But she won't and neither will the rest of us. We wouldn't come to your party if it was the last party on the face of the earth."

Krista appeared by Lori's side. "You must be Katie! You sound just like—" she stopped abruptly. In the silence that followed, Megan could hear the unspoken words that would have finished the sentence. *Just like Megan described you,* or something like that.

"Who are *you?*" Katie asked.

"Krista."

Sarah got into it. "Oh, yeah. Megan's so-called best friend."

Krista shrank back.

Lori seemed to be not at all bothered by the tension in the air. "Well, it's too bad that you can't come. You'll be missing a great time."

Anger churned inside Megan. She could see what Lori was trying to do. She wanted to win over Megan's Sunnyside friends too!

But they weren't going to fall for Lori's tricks. Trina spoke calmly and politely. "Thank you for your invitation, Lori. But we're here to visit our friend Megan. And if Megan isn't invited to your party, we don't want to come either."

87

Lori cocked her head to one side. "Actually, Megan *could* come. On one condition."

Megan couldn't resist asking. "What condition?"

"You know the empty house across the street from me? You have to go in it, all by yourself, after dark, and spend twenty minutes inside."

Megan could hear Julie's gasp. "You want her to go inside the haunted house?"

"That's ridiculous," Katie fumed. "She doesn't have to do that."

"Of course, she doesn't *have* to," Lori replied. "And I know she won't. She'd be much too scared. I've heard about Megan's nightmares."

She was talking as if Megan wasn't even there. But that wasn't what made Megan's anger turn into fury. Of her friends here in town, only Krista knew about the nightmares Megan used to have whenever she saw a scary movie or read a scary book. Krista had told Lori about this. She'd betrayed her former best friend. And now Lori would tell everyone that Megan was a whimpering, frightened baby.

"She wouldn't be scared," Sarah said.

"That's not even the point," Katie argued. "You're acting as if she *wants* to come to your dumb party."

But she *did* want to come. For two weeks, Megan had felt left out, excluded, lonely. It was great having her cabin six friends here, but when they left on Sunday, she'd be alone again. This was her chance to get back together with her friends, to make them listen to her and realize she wasn't the bad person Lori had made them believe she was.

"Just forget it, Lori," Katie continued. "Megan doesn't need you or any of your stupid friends."

"Wait," Megan said suddenly. Now all eyes were on her. She took a deep breath. "I'll do it."

For the first time, Lori's sneering expression disappeared, and she looked at Megan blankly. "You will?"

Megan nodded.

"Really? You can't just say you did it, you know. We'll be watching from across the street. With binoculars. And you'll have to take a flashlight with you, and shine it in each window, so we'll know you went to every room."

Megan tried to swallow, but there was a huge lump in her throat. In her mind, she could see that second story window again, lit up, and the figure of the ghost. She clutched her hands together tightly so no one could see them tremble.

"All right."

Lori's voice became businesslike. "Okay, let's

89

see. The party starts at eight o'clock. Krista and Julie and Paige will come over early, and we'll be watching for you to go into the house at seven-thirty."

Megan nodded in agreement. Behind Lori, she saw Krista, looking pale and uncomfortable. "Lori, we don't feel much like playing anymore. Let's go."

"Okay," Lori said. "See you all tomorrow!"

The cabin six girls were silent until the other girls left. "What haunted house?" Erin asked.

Megan explained. "There's an old, run-down house across from Lori's. It's been empty for almost a year. They say that sometimes, at night, a light goes on upstairs and the ghost of a woman looks out."

"But you don't believe that, do you?" Trina asked.

Megan managed a feeble smile. "I saw it."

A sharp intake of breath came from Sarah. Katie looked skeptical, but Trina shuddered and Erin grimaced.

Sarah laid a gentle hand on Megan's arm. "Do you really want to go to that party so much?"

"I hope you're not doing this for us," Trina added.

"Yeah, I don't mind missing the party," Erin said. "I mean, I'd *like* to go, but—"

"It's not the party," Megan interrupted. "Look, right now, no one's even speaking to me. If I'm at the party, they'll have to start talking to me again. And maybe we can straighten this whole mess out."

"We'll go in the house with you," Katie stated.

Erin made a face. "Speak for yourself. *I'm* not going into any haunted house."

"You can't anyway," Megan told them. "You heard what Lori said. They'll be watching, and I have to go in alone."

"Wait," Trina said. "I just thought of something. You can't just walk into a house, even if it's abandoned. It's against the law, isn't it?"

"That's right," Sarah agreed. "It's trespassing."

"Well, that settles that," Katie said. "You can't break the law."

Megan heaved a huge sigh of relief. "I didn't think of that. You're right. I'm not about to go to jail, not for Lori Landers and her Halloween party."

"You wouldn't go to jail," Erin argued. "They don't put kids in jail. Besides, I don't think it's against the law to just walk into a house, as long as you're not planning to rob it. I walk into my best friend's house all the time. I think it's okay, as long as you knock first."

"Hey, maybe that's right," Katie said. "Megan, before you go in, knock at the door. And if nobody answers—"

"When nobody answers," Sarah corrected her. "The house is abandoned, remember?"

Katie grinned. "Maybe the ghost will open the door."

Trina shot her a disapproving look. "Don't joke about it. No one's going to open the door—not even Megan. The house is probably locked up tight."

"Not necessarily." Megan sighed. "Some teenagers broke into the house a while back and damaged the front door lock. I remember my parents talking about how no one could get hold of the owners to have it fixed, and how dangerous it was. I bet it's still broken."

"I guess we won't know till we try it," Katie said.

"Till *I* try it," Megan muttered.

Erin got up. "Well, if we're going to a Halloween party, I'm going to need a costume. Lori said there's a place that rents costumes right down the block."

Megan rose. "Yeah, maybe I'll rent one too. I

don't want to spend a lot of time making something. Have we finished the game?"

They hadn't, but no one felt much like playing anymore. They started toward the place where they'd turned in their shoes. Megan lagged behind, and Sarah stayed with her.

"Megan, you don't *have* to do this. I know you're not afraid of scary movies anymore, and personally, I don't believe in ghosts, but an empty old house . . . that can be kind of creepy."

Megan nodded fervently. "But it's the only way. Unless—Katie?"

Katie turned. "Yeah?"

"I don't suppose you've come up with one of your brilliant schemes to help me out, have you?"

Katie hung her head. "Not yet."

Megan gave Sarah a halfhearted, trembling smile. "Then it looks like I'm going to be meeting a ghost."

Chapter 8

"How do I look?" Katie asked.

"Wow!" Trina replied. "That's fantastic! Where did you find a pirate costume?"

"My mother made it for a play one of my brothers was in two years ago. I found it in the attic." Katie studied herself in the mirror, and pulled on the eyepatch that covered one eye. "But it needs something. I know! Erin, let me borrow your black pencil thing."

"It's called an eyeliner," Erin said. "I better show you how to use it."

Katie snatched the eyeliner from her. "I *know* how I'm going to use it." Leaning closer to the mirror, she drew a black line above her lip.

"You're ruining the point!" Erin wailed, but Katie ignored her as she admired her moustache.

"That's outrageous!" Sarah exclaimed. "Erin, what are you supposed to be?"

Erin smoothed the front of the soft pink chiffon gown, and adjusted the gold-colored tiara on her head. "A princess, of course."

Sarah nudged Megan. "That sounds typical, right?"

Megan smiled wanly and nodded. She'd been sitting cross-legged on her bed, watching and listening as the others prepared themselves for Halloween. But she hadn't even started getting ready herself.

Normally, she'd be enjoying all this frantic activity. In a way, it was like old times at Camp Sunnyside, with everyone running around the cabin and excited about some special event. She wished she could relax and join in.

She made an effort. "Trina, you look cool."

"Thanks," Trina said. "But even in this costume, I don't think I look much like a witch."

Megan had to agree with that. Trina's face was just too sweet to make a convincingly mean witch. "You can always be a good witch, like in *The Wizard of Oz.*"

"Not with this mask," Katie said. She picked up the rubber face, with its huge nose and disgusting warts.

"At least it's better than last year's costume,"

Trina said. "All I wore last year was an old white sheet with holes cut out for eyes. I was supposed to be a ghost, but—" She stopped abruptly. All eyes automatically turned to Megan, and then just as quickly turned away.

Megan got off her bed. "It's okay. I don't believe in ghosts."

"But you said you saw one looking out the window of that house," Erin reminded her. She was busily applying big red spots of rouge to Sarah's cheeks.

"It was probably just my imagination," Megan replied. She didn't sound very convincing, not even to herself.

But the others pretended to agree. "You're right," Katie said. "We know how you daydream."

"Absolutely," Sarah said. "It was all in your mind."

Only Erin didn't go along. "Are you sure? Okay, Megan has a wild imagination. But you don't usually go around seeing things that aren't there, do you?"

"Okay, here's another explanation," Trina said quickly. "You said that some kids had broken into the house. Maybe they've been sneaking in at night and hanging out there."

For a moment, Megan felt hopeful. "Hey,

that's possible. I just hope they aren't there when I go in."

Sarah fluffed out the ruffle around the neck of her clown costume. "It's after seven, Megan. You better get into your costume."

"Yeah, I guess I can't put it off any longer." Megan went to the closet and took out the bag from the costume rental store.

Erin shook her head with disapproval as Megan pulled out the glittery dress. "I still don't think that's very smart, Megan. Wearing the same costume as Lori."

"She might think it's funny," Sarah said. "If she has a sense of humor." The words "which I doubt" hung in the air, unspoken.

"Or maybe she'll take it as a compliment," Trina noted brightly.

Megan didn't care one way or another. "There's nothing I can do about it now." Her voice was muffled as she pulled the dress over her head. "This was the only costume they had left in my size."

Trina glanced out the window. "We're lucky the weather turned warm. I guess this is what they call an Indian summer. We won't have to cover our costumes with coats."

Megan scrutinized her reflection in the mirror. "Personally, I think this would look *better* covered with a coat."

"Put the wig on," Sarah encouraged her. She helped Megan stuff her curls under the wild pink wig. "Isn't there a mask that goes with this too?"

"Yeah." Megan took it out of the bag and tried it on. "Ick, it itches." She pulled it down so it hung around her neck. Then she shivered.

"Are you scared?" Trina asked.

Megan knew there was no point in lying to these guys. "Yes."

Sarah gazed at her seriously. "You can still back out."

Megan shook her head. "I won't give Lori the satisfaction of thinking I'm a wimp."

"It won't be so bad," Katie reassured her. "We'll all be outside, standing guard."

Megan eyed her nervously. "What do you think you're guarding me from?"

"Well, I don't know Lori but I know her type. It's not enough that you're going into that house. She's got some sort of scheme, and we're going to be prepared for whatever it is. Now, have you got the flashlight?"

"Yeah." Megan looked at the clock, and pulled on her mask. "Come on, let's go."

But first they had to pass through the living

room, where Megan's parents were sitting. Baby Alex took one look at them and burst into tears.

"Good grief!" Mr. Lindsay cried out. "Who are those creatures who have invaded our home?"

Mrs. Lindsay was comforting Alex. "You girls look absolutely adorable. Now, where are you going?"

"To a party," Megan replied.

"Where?"

She was glad the mask hid her expression. "At Lori Landers'."

Her mother was understandably surprised. "Really?" Then she pulled Megan aside. "I'm so pleased, honey. And I'm proud of you for working out your differences."

She thinks everything's fine and dandy, Megan thought miserably. Well, maybe by tomorrow she'd deserve her mother's praise. If she survived tonight.

With her parents' cries of "have a good time" ringing in their ears, Megan and her friends left the house. Megan immediately pulled off the itchy mask.

Up and down the street, small groups of ghosts, witches, cowboys, and unidentifiable creatures roamed from house to house. Passing Krista's home, Megan wondered if Krista's mother was passing out her delicious home-made butterscotch brownies.

Sarah paused before one house to watch a group of kids accept their treats. "Ooh, candy apples. Couldn't we—"

"No time," Katie said.

Trina and Sarah kept up a steady stream of chatter, pointing out cute trick-or-treaters and remarking on their costumes. Megan barely heard them. As they turned the corner to the street where the abandoned house stood, she felt her heartbeat quicken. They passed the church and then the cemetery. Funny, Megan thought. During the day, it looked so pretty. Now, in the darkness, it was eerie.

And then they were nearing the house.

"Is that it?" Erin asked. She shuddered. "Gross. It looks really creepy."

"Shut up, Erin," Katie snapped. "It's just an old house, that's all."

"That's Lori's house, across the street," Megan pointed out.

"It feels weird," Sarah said. "Knowing they'll be watching us."

"Not us," Megan said glumly. "Me."

"Yeah," Katie said. "And we can't let them see us. We'd better go around by the side of the house."

But no one moved right away. "I hate leaving you here all alone," Trina said to Megan.

Megan squared her shoulders and raised her head. "It's okay, guys. I can handle it." She was impressed with how brave she sounded. If only she *felt* that way.

Katie's voice dropped to a whisper. "All right, you guys. Let's go."

Megan watched as they walked in single file up the untended lawn to the side of the house. As they disappeared from view, she felt very much alone.

Somehow, she willed her legs to move. With a steadfast gait, she made her way toward the front door of the house. Glancing up, she caught her breath.

Did she see a light flicker in the upstairs window and then go off? Or was her imagination playing tricks on her?

Megan had an urge to turn and run back to the road. But knowing the girls across the street were watching through binoculars, she didn't even want her expression to reveal what she was feeling.

She steeled herself to look up again. Now the window was dark. Maybe her eyes had just played a trick on her.

She put her mask back on. Even though it

itched, she felt like it gave her some protection. But protection from what? She didn't want to think about that.

She reached the door and put her hand on the doorknob. For one brief, fleeting moment, she hoped the door would be locked. But it wasn't. The knob turned easily, and the door opened with an ominous groan.

A lamp from the street provided a slight glimmer of light inside, just enough for Megan to see where she was going. But she switched on her flashlight anyway. First, she aimed it at her watch. It was exactly 7:32. Twenty minutes, Lori had said. That meant she could leave at precisely 7:52. She didn't plan to spend one more minute in that house than was necessary.

She directed the beam of light around the hallway. There was nothing there, except for some cobwebs and lots of dust. Slowly, she turned to the room on the left. Before she went in, she swept the light around. It was empty.

She walked in, went directly to a window, and shone the flashlight on it. She hoped the girls across the street could see through the grimy glass.

She turned and went back across the hallway and into the opposite room. That room was empty too. Once again, she went to a window and flashed the light.

So far, it had been easy. She was beginning to feel like this wasn't going to be such an ordeal after all. But now it was time to go upstairs, before her courage could evaporate.

As she mounted the steps, they let out creaks that filled the silent house with noise. She paused halfway, to peer up at the landing. There, while standing absolutely still, she heard another creak.

Her heart started pounding again. Where had that creak come from? Gripping the rail, somehow she made it up the rest of the stairs.

She was in a hallway. Three rooms led off of it. Which should she visit first? she wondered.

Her eyes kept drifting to the room on the left. That would be the one the light had come from. She might as well get that one over with.

Taking a deep breath, she edged toward it. She lifted her flashlight. But she didn't need it. Without any warning, the entire room lit up.

Her brain told her to run. But her legs weren't taking any commands. Only her eyes moved— to the window where the ghost always appeared.

The form of the woman was there. Only it wasn't a woman at all. It was just a torso, without arms or legs or head. She'd seen one just like it before, when she went with her mother to see a seamstress.

A dressmaker's dummy, set just back from a window. That's all it was.

She was so relieved she almost smiled. But there was still something weird going on here, something she didn't understand. The light. Who had turned it on?

Then she spotted something on the wall by the door that gave her the answer. They had one exactly like it at home. It was an automatic light timer. Her father had installed it so that lights would go on in the living room even when no one was home.

Now she *did* smile. She almost started laughing. All those stories about ghosts and mysterious lights—and this was the explanation. Whoever had lived here didn't disconnect the timer when he left. The batteries were probably wearing out, and that was why the light went on for just a minute or so now and then. And the left-behind dummy made it appear that a woman was standing behind the window.

The room went dark. But now, Megan was feeling practically lighthearted. This was going to make a great story to tell when she got to the party.

Then she heard something.

It wasn't her imagination. It was a noise . . . no, a voice. But there were no words, just a sound, like someone moaning. And groaning. It was coming from one of the other rooms or maybe from downstairs.

Megan was totally paralyzed. She gripped her flashlight tightly, but she couldn't bring herself to turn around.

The groaning stopped, but that wasn't the end of the voice. It started to laugh, a laugh that was more like a cackle. Then the laughter turned into a high-pitched wailing. It seemed to go on forever. But when the wailing stopped, she heard something even worse.

Her name. "Megan. Megan." And then, "Get out. Get out."

Suddenly, she understood. And she wasn't afraid anymore.

It was a trick. It was a silly, childish game. Somewhere in this house, Lori was groaning, laughing, wailing, calling Megan's name. Maybe Krista, Julie, and Paige were doing it too.

Should she go in search of them? She turned, moved out into the hall, and looked at the room to the right. Someone was coming out.

Megan held up the flashlight. The figure in

the long, gypsy skirt gasped. Then she relaxed. "Whew, you startled me," Krista said. "I thought you were downstairs. I'm glad you stopped making those noises. You were giving *me* the creeps."

She thinks I'm Lori, Megan realized. They must not have seen me when I came into the house. Hesitantly, she touched her mask, to make sure it was still there.

"Where's Megan?" Krista asked.

Megan didn't trust herself to speak. Her voice might give her away. She just shrugged.

"Maybe she's already run out of the house," Krista said. Then she sighed. "Lori, I really don't like doing this. Don't get me wrong, I'm still mad at Megan. I was really upset when you told us that awful stuff she was saying about me and Paige and Julie. It's still hard for me to believe. Megan was my best friend. But right now I feel so . . . *mean.*"

From another room, Paige and Julie emerged. "I guess we scared her off," Julie said. She didn't sound very happy about it.

I'll bet she was really freaked out," Paige added.

Krista bit her lip, and turned to Lori. "I never should have told you about how Megan used to have nightmares."

There was the sound of soft footsteps on the stairs. "Shh, she's coming!" Julie hissed. The three of them ran back into the room they'd come out of. Megan went back into the other room, and switched off the flashlight.

A figure appeared at the door. It wore a glitter dress, a pink wig, and a mask. "Krista, why did you—"

Before she could finish, Megan switched the flashlight back on.

And Lori screamed.

Chapter 9

Megan jerked off her mask. "Relax, Lori. It's me."

For once, Lori was totally speechless.

"Isn't your mask itchy?" Megan asked.

Lori pulled hers off. Her face was pale, but her eyes were narrowed into tiny hard slits.

Megan spoke casually. "I knew you were good at tennis, Lori. But I didn't know you had so many other talents."

Lori found her voice. "What do you mean?"

"You're very good at moaning and groaning. And that laugh was just super."

Lori seemed to be struggling to regain her composure, but her efforts were in vain. Her voice was shaky. "I don't know what you're talking about."

All the misery of the past two weeks rushed through Megan's mind, and she let it out. "Lori,

why are you doing this to me? Not just this . . ."
She waved her hand, indicating the house. "Everything! Ever since you came to town, you've done anything you could think of to ruin my life!"

Lori placed her hands on her hips. "Yeah? Well, you ruined *mine!*"

That comment took Megan aback. "What are *you* talking about?"

Lori's face went pink. "I was the best tennis player around. My parents were so proud of me. They thought I'd become a professional player, and so did I. That's all I ever dreamed about, all I hoped for. Then you beat me at the tournament. In front of my parents and all my friends. And that was the end of everything for me."

Megan couldn't believe her ears. "That's crazy! Even the best tennis players in the world lose a game once in a while!"

"Well, *I* never lost a game before," Lori shot back. "After you beat me, I told my parents I was through with tennis. I'd never play again. If I can't be the best, what's the point?"

It took Megan a moment to comprehend what she was saying. When she finally figured it out, she said, "That's the dumbest thing I've ever heard in my life." She remembered a saying her father liked. "It's—it's cutting off your nose to spite your face."

Lori obviously had never heard that saying before. "Huh?"

"Well, you're sad because you lost that game. So you give up tennis, which just makes you even sadder. I'll bet you miss playing tennis, don't you?"

Lori shrugged.

"Oh, come on, Lori. Think about it. Tearing across the court, whacking the ball, watching it clear the net, waiting to see what kind of return you're going to get. Tell the truth, Lori. You miss playing tennis."

Lori didn't respond. But Megan thought she saw the glimmer of tears in her eyes.

So she went on. "You were lying when you said you didn't care about tennis anymore. Just like you lied to Krista and Julie and Paige about me. You took what I told you about them, twisted it around, and made it sound like I was saying something nasty. You got everyone in class thinking I'm awful. And all just to get even with me for beating you in one crummy game."

Megan paused for a breath. She felt as if she'd just given a long speech, a lecture—like something parents and teachers would do. If Lori hated her before, there was no telling how she must feel about her now. But at least Megan felt better.

Krista, Paige, and Julie appeared in the doorway. Their eyes darted back and forth between Megan and Lori. Then Krista spoke. "We heard what Megan said. Is it true, Lori? Did you lie to us?"

Megan held her breath. It seemed like an eternity passed before Lori nodded. And then there was silence.

It was broken by a sound, that seemed to come from downstairs. Julie clutched Paige's arm. "What was that?"

"It—it sounds like a bird," Paige replied.

"A bird?" Lori started to shake. "Is it a bird?"

It was a loud *caw-caw,* like a huge crow's. And it was getting louder. Megan knew what it was. She grinned.

Lori burst into tears. "Keep it away! Keep it away! It's something awful! It's going to get us!"

Her voice rose with each sentence. She's hysterical, Megan thought. She ran over and put her hands on Lori's shoulders. "Lori, calm down! It's okay! It's not really a bird!" Over her shoulder, she yelled, "Trina, cut it out!"

The bird sound stopped. A moment later, Trina, Katie, Sarah, and Erin burst into the room.

Lori was still sobbing uncontrollably. "What's wrong with her?" Erin asked.

"She doesn't like birds," Megan said.

Katie grinned. "Good."

"Don't say that, Katie," Megan scolded. "She's really upset." She stroked Lori's head. "It's okay, Lori. There aren't any birds. It was just Trina, doing bird calls."

Finally, Lori's tears subsided, but she was still sniffling. "Does anyone have a tissue?" Megan asked.

Even in a witch costume, Trina was prepared. She dug into a pocket and handed Lori a fresh tissue.

Lori wiped her eyes and blew her nose. Then, as if she'd just realized what she'd been doing, her face went red and she looked wretchedly embarrassed.

"Are you okay?" Krista asked nervously.

Lori nodded. "I . . . look, I guess I went a little crazy. It's just that . . . I've always had this thing about birds. Ever since I saw this movie . . ." Her voice trailed off.

Julie giggled, but she stopped when Megan looked at her sharply. "Don't laugh at her. I know what it's like. Once, I saw a movie about a typical teenaged girl who was really a witch.

112

And I got the idea that one of the campers at Sunnyside was a witch. Remember?"

"I remember," Trina said, smiling.

"Me too," Erin chimed in. "You really made a fool of yourself, Megan."

Megan disregarded the insult. "See, everybody's got something that freaks her out."

Lori looked at her in wonderment. "Why are you defending me? After the way I've acted to you . . ."

"No kidding," Krista blurted out. She sounded as if *she* were about to burst into tears. "You made me hate my best friend. Megan, I'm sorry. Can you forgive me?"

Megan hesitated. The past few weeks had been a nightmare that she wouldn't forget quickly. She felt too sorry for Lori now to be angry at her. But Krista? Krista had been her best friend, someone who was supposed to stick by her through thick and thin. It was going to be a lot harder to forgive *her.*

Then the light in the room came on again. While Erin shrieked and everyone else gasped, Megan got a good look at Krista's face. She *was* crying. Real tears were trickling down her face, and Megan knew she wasn't faking it.

Megan melted. She couldn't stand seeing Krista cry. One day soon, she'd sit down privately with Krista and tell her how awful this had been. They could have a real heart-to-heart talk about it, and they'd be best friends again.

But right now, all she could do was say the thing that would make Krista feel better. As the light went out, she spoke.

"I forgive you."

"Us too?" Paige asked.

"You too."

Katie spoke up. "I think there's someone else who should say she's sorry." She looked pointedly at Lori.

Lori raised her head. "I'm sorry, Megan."

Megan believed her. "I'll forgive you, Lori. On one condition."

Lori looked almost a little frightened. "What's that?"

"Play tennis with me next Saturday."

Lori's lips twitched. Then she actually smiled. "Okay."

Erin nudged Megan. "You see? I told you she was cool."

"Hey, you guys," Julie said. "Do you realize we're in the room where the ghost is?"

"There's no ghost," Megan announced. "Look." With her flashlight, she showed them the automatic timer. "That's what makes the lights go on." She moved the beam to the dressmaker's dummy. "And there's your ghost, Julie."

Julie studied the figure. "Well, it *is* headless." Then she started giggling. Paige joined in. And within seconds they were all laughing.

"Ohmigosh," Lori exclaimed. "It's eight o'clock! My party!" They all ran downstairs and out of the house. As they crossed the street, Katie explained the bird calls.

"We were watching from the side of the house, and we saw you guys go in. I figured you had some sort of scheme to scare Megan. So we decided to follow you in and pull a trick on you."

"Pretty smart," Lori admitted. "I have to admit, your scheme worked better than ours. Who made the bird calls?"

"That was me," Trina said, with a combination of embarrassment and pride. "I wouldn't have done it if I'd known you had a real fear of birds."

"I thought it sounded neat," Julie said. "Can you teach me how to do those sounds?"

"Julie!" Lori yelped. "Don't you dare!"

"It's something we could threaten you with if you ever start acting obnoxious again," Krista said.

Lori stiffened. Then she sighed and gave them all an abashed grin. "Okay, I've been a jerk.

Are you guys going to hold it against me forever?"

"I don't think they will," Katie said. "Even
Megan acts like a jerk sometimes, but we Sunnyside girls don't hold it against her."

"Even Megan?" Sarah interjected. "What
about even *you?*"

Katie threw back her head and laughed.

"Oh, Megan," Krista said, putting an arm
around her. "I'm so glad that's all over with.
I've missed you."

"I've missed you too," Megan said promptly.

Lori's eyes roamed the group, and then she
turned to Megan. "You know, you're lucky to
have such good friends."

Megan looked around. "Yes, you're right. I *am*
lucky to have such good friends." She grinned
at Lori.

"But I can always use one more."

MEET THE GIRLS FROM CABIN SIX IN

CAMP SUNNYSIDE FRIENDS

(#13) BIG SISTER BLUES	76551-9	($2.95 US/$3.50 Can)
(#12) THE TENNIS TRAP	76184-X	($2.95 US/$3.50 Can)
(#11) THE PROBLEM WITH PARENTS		
	76183-1	($2.95 US/$3.50 Can)
(#10) ERIN AND THE MOVIE STAR	76181-5	($2.95 US/$3.50 Can)
(#9) THE NEW-AND-IMPROVED SARAH		
	76180-7	($2.95 US/$3.50 Can)
(#8) TOO MANY COUNSELORS	75913-6	($2.95 US/$3.50 Can)
(#7) A WITCH IN CABIN SIX	75912-8	($2.95 US/$3.50 Can)
(#6) KATIE STEALS THE SHOW	75910-1	($2.95 US/$3.50 Can)
(#5) LOOKING FOR TROUBLE	75909-8	($2.95 US/$3.50 Can)
(#4) NEW GIRL IN CABIN SIX	75703-6	($2.95 US/$3.50 Can)
(#3) COLOR WAR!	75702-8	($2.50 US/$2.95 Can)
(#2) CABIN SIX PLAYS CUPID	75701-X	($2.50 US/$2.95 Can)
(#1) NO BOYS ALLOWED!	75700-1	($2.50 US/$2.95 Can)
MY CAMP MEMORY BOOK	76081-9	($5.95 US/$7.95 Can)

CAMP SUNNYSIDE FRIENDS SPECIAL:
CHRISTMAS REUNION　　　　76270-6 ($2.95 US/$3.50 Can)

Buy these books at your local bookstore or use this coupon for ordering:

Mail to: Avon Books, Dept BP, Box 767, Rte 2, Dresden, TN 38225
Please send me the book(s) I have checked above.
☐ My check or money order—no cash or CODs please—for $_____ is enclosed
(please add $1.00 to cover postage and handling for each book ordered to a maximum of
three dollars—Canadian residents add 7% GST).
☐ Charge my VISA/MC Acct#_____ Exp Date _____
Phone No _____ I am ordering a minimum of two books (please add
postage and handling charge of $2.00 plus 50 cents per title after the first two books to a
maximum of six dollars—Canadian residents add 7% GST). For faster service, call 1-800-
762-0779. Residents of Tennessee, please call 1-800-633-1607. Prices and numbers are
subject to change without notice. Please allow six to eight weeks for delivery.

Name _____

Address _____

City _____ State/Zip _____

SUN　0891

A CAST OF CHARACTERS
TO DELIGHT THE HEARTS
OF READERS!

BUNNICULA   **51094-4/$2.95 U.S./$3.50 CAN.**
James and Deborah Howe, illustrated by Alan Daniel
The now-famous story of the vampire bunny, this ALA
Notable Book begins the light-hearted story of the small
rabbit the Monroe family find in a shoebox at a Dracula
film. He looks like any ordinary bunny to Harold the dog.
But Chester, a well-read and observant cat, is suspicious
of the newcomer, whose teeth strangely resemble
fangs...

HOWLIDAY INN   **69294-5/$3.50 U.S./$3.95 CAN.**
James Howe, illustrated by Lynn Munsinger
The continued "tail" of Chester the cat and Harold the dog
as they spend their summer vacation at the foreboding
Chateau Bow-Wow, a kennel run by a mad scientist!

THE CELERY STALKS   **69054-3/$2.95 U.S./$3.50 CAN.**
AT MIDNIGHT
James Howe, illustrated by Leslie Morrill
Bunnicula is back and on the loose in this third hilarious
novel featuring Chester the cat, Harold the dog, and the
famous vampire bunny.

NIGHTY-NIGHTMARE   **70490-0/$3.50 U.S./$3.95 CAN.**
James Howe, illustrated by Leslie Morrill
Join Chester the cat, Harold the dog, and Howie the other
family dog as they hear the tale of how Bunnicula was
born while they are on an overnight camping trip full of
surprises!

Buy these books at your local bookstore or use this coupon for ordering:
....
Mail to: Avon Books, Dept BP, Box 767, Rte 2, Dresden, TN 38225
Please send me the book(s) I have checked above.
☐ My check or money order—no cash or CODs please—for $_____ is enclosed
(please add $1.00 to cover postage and handling for each book ordered to a maximum of
three dollars—Canadian residents add 7% GST).
☐ Charge my VISA/MC Acct# _____ Exp Date _____
Phone No _____ I am ordering a minimum of two books (please add
postage and handling charge of $2.00 plus 50 cents per title after the first two books to a
maximum of six dollars—Canadian residents add 7% GST). For faster service, call 1-800-
762-0779. Residents of Tennessee, please call 1-800-633-1607. Prices and numbers are
subject to change without notice. Please allow six to eight weeks for delivery.

Name _____

Address _____

City _____ State/Zip _____.

HOW   0391

EXTRA! EXTRA!
Read All About It in...

THE
TREEHOUSE
TIMES

(#9) STINKY BUSINESS

76269-2 ($2.95 US/$3.50 Can)

(#8) THE GREAT RIP-OFF

75902-0 ($2.95 US/$3.50 Can)

(#7) RATS! 75901-2 ($2.95 US/$3.50 Can)

(#6) THE PRESS MESS

75900-4 ($2.95 US/$3.50 Can)

(#5) DAPHNE TAKES CHARGE

75899-7 ($2.95 US/$3.50 Can)

(#4) FIRST COURSE: TROUBLE

75783-4 ($2.50 US/$2.95 Can)

(#3) SPAGHETTI BREATH

75782-6 ($2.50 US/$2.95 Can)

(#2) THE KICKBALL CRISIS

75781-8 ($2.50 US/$2.95 Can)

(#1) UNDER 12 NOT ALLOWED

75780-X ($2.50 US/$2.95 Can)

AVON Camelot Paperbacks

Buy these books at your local bookstore or use this coupon for ordering:

Mail to: Avon Books, Dept BP, Box 767, Rte 2, Dresden, TN 38225
Please send me the book(s) I have checked above.
⌐ My check or money order—no cash or CODs please—for $_____ is enclosed
(please add $1.00 to cover postage and handling for each book ordered to a maximum of
three dollars—Canadian residents add 7% GST).
⌐ Charge my VISA/MC Acct#_____ Exp Date _____
Phone No _____ I am ordering a minimum of two books (please add
postage and handling charge of $2.00 plus 50 cents per title after the first two books to a
maximum of six dollars—Canadian residents add 7% GST). For faster service, call 1-800-
762-0779. Residents of Tennessee, please call 1-800-633-1607. Prices and numbers are
subject to change without notice. Please allow six to eight weeks for delivery.

Name_____

Address_____

City _____ State/Zip _____

TRE   0391

WORLDS OF WONDER
FROM
AVON CAMELOT

THE INDIAN IN THE CUPBOARD
60012-9/$3.25US/$3.95Can

THE RETURN OF THE INDIAN
70284-3/$3.50US only

Lynne Reid Banks

"Banks conjures up a story that is both thoughtful and captivating and interweaves the fantasy with care and believability" *Booklist*

THE HUNKY-DORY DAIRY
Anne Lindbergh   70320-3/$2.95US/$3.75Can

"A beguiling fantasy...full of warmth, wit and charm"
Kirkus Reviews

THE MAGIC OF THE GLITS
C.S. Adler   70403-X/$2.50US/$3.25Can

"A truly magical book" *The Reading Teacher*

GOOD-BYE PINK PIG
C.S. Adler   70175-8/$2.75US/$3.25 Can

Every fifth grader needs a friend she can count on!

Buy these books at your local bookstore or use this coupon for ordering:

Mail to: Avon Books, Dept BP, Box 767, Rte 2, Dresden, TN 38225
Please send me the book(s) I have checked above.
☐ My check or money order—no cash or CODs please—for $ _____ is enclosed
(please add $1.00 to cover postage and handling for each book ordered to a maximum of
three dollars—Canadian residents add 7% GST).
☐ Charge my VISA/MC Acct# _____ Exp Date _____
Phone No _____ I am ordering a minimum of two books (please add
postage and handling charge of $2.00 plus 50 cents per title after the first two books to a
maximum of six dollars—Canadian residents add 7% GST). For faster service, call 1-800-
762-0779. Residents of Tennessee, please call 1-800-633-1607. Prices and numbers are
subject to change without notice. Please allow six to eight weeks for delivery.

Name _____

Address _____

City _____ State/Zip _____

WON 0391